IRISH WHISKEY

IT'S ALL IN THE WHISKEY, BOOK 8

JEN TALTY

JUPITER PRESS

Irish Whiskey left his cousins' farm years ago to join the Army and he never looked back. That was until he gets a phone call from one of his relatives informing him that one of the many broken hearts he left behind showed up at Whiskey Ranch claiming to be carrying his child.

And she won't leave until he comes back and decides if he wants to be a father, or he's going to do what he's always done—run from his responsibilities.

Lorelei Sheldon knew the second the sexy Special Forces officer walked into her diner she was in trouble. But she hadn't expected it to be the kind of trouble that would change the course of her entire life. With no way of reaching him, except through his family's ranch in Buhl, Idaho, Lorelei packs up her things and sets off to find the man who she knows without a doubt she wants to start a life with, but also understands he might want nothing to do with her.

But she has to try. She owes it to their unborn child.

IRISH WHISKEY

IT'S ALL IN THE WHISKEY BOOK 8

USA Today Bestselling Author
JEN TALTY

*Sign up for my Newsletter
(https://dl.bookfunnel.com/82gm8b9k4y) where I often
give away free books before publication.*

*Join my private Facebook group (https://www.facebook.
com/groups/191706547909047/) where I post exclusive
excerpts and discuss all things murder and love!*

Never miss a new release. Follow me on
Amazon:amazon.com/author/jentalty
And on Bookbub: bookbub.com/authors/jen-talty

*I*rish Whiskey shoved the gearshift of his Jeep into park with a little too much force than necessary. He let out a long breath as he stared off into the night. He'd been stateside maybe sixty days of the entire year and he was getting damn tired of jumping from perfectly good airplanes, especially when he hadn't a fucking clue half the time if he was going to actually land his feet in hostile or friendly territory.

"Come on, man. You're the one who started this ritual. Let's go," Gunny, his best friend, said as he parked his honking brand-new shiny bright-red pickup truck right next to Irish's dated Jeep. But hey, it was in mint condition, with low mileage, and he planned on driving it until he died.

"I'm coming." Irish and Gunny had been on the

same team now for six years and Gunny was about as gung ho as anyone could be about the Army. He reminded Irish of how he used to be when he'd first joined. Or even just a few years ago when every assignment made his pulse race with excitement.

Bright-eyed and bushy-tailed with ants in his pants and not a care in the fucking world.

That's what his cousin JW Whiskey used to say about him when Irish hightailed it off the family ranch when he'd been eighteen years old. JW also accused Irish of running from his responsibilities, which was only partially true. The ranch wasn't his, nor was it his father's. It was JW's and his siblings and while Irish would have been given a place at the ranch for life, he still didn't feel bad about leaving.

Well, not really.

But the bigger issue had been his father and his depression after his mother had run off with one of the cowboys training at Whiskey Ranch.

She'd been cheating on Irish's father for as long as he could remember and her leaving should have been a blessing, but his father could never get over it.

Not that he'd tried all that hard.

But that wasn't Irish's problem. Nor could he stop his father from drinking himself to death and that wasn't something that Irish wanted to sit around and watch.

Which is exactly what the old man did less than a year after Irish left.

As for his mama, well, he hadn't spoken to her in nearly fifteen years and he had no plans on reaching out anytime soon.

"I might have started it, but if you recall, I was the one who suggested we forget the whole thing." Irish stepped from his vehicle and the warm North Carolina summer air assaulted his face. He liked the state but not so much Fort Bragg. It had been a while since he'd been to the Army base. Eight years, to be exact.

And he hadn't missed it.

"Except at zero eight hundred, our asses have to be in the briefing room and who knows how long this next mission is going to be. And I have it on good authority that a sexy young lady I know could be here tonight."

"Someone you actually know? Or are you just checking things out?" A year ago, Irish would have been on the prowl as well, but at thirty-three, he was damn tired of women he couldn't remember that blended into a long string of meaningless one-night stands.

There had to be more to life than what he'd been doing, only he didn't know anything else.

Not anymore.

But he was about to find out since he missed the cutoff to sign his re-enlistment papers and when he returned from this mission, he'd no longer be a lieutenant in the Army.

A fact he refused to let very few people know.

"You can't tell anyone, because I don't need to be harassed, but I've been sort of corresponding with someone."

"Good for you." He slapped his buddy on the back. "This place sure has changed." He glanced around the packed parking lot. The last time he'd been at Lucky Charms Diner had been right after Ranger training. It had been a beat-up old diner that happened to also be a damn good bar. He'd gotten so shit-faced he could barely piece together the evening.

Not that it mattered and there wouldn't be a repeat.

Nope. Those days were long gone.

He'd get his food, have a couple of beers, and then go to his pathetic place of an apartment before grabbing an hour or two of sleep.

"This place is hopping." Gunny bounced up and down like a kid in a candy store. He turned his head left and right, scanning, obviously looking for whoever he'd been secretly communicating with.

Irish kept his laughter, and his opinion, to himself. Gunny wouldn't be the first soldier to have a girl he kept to himself.

"Welcome to Lucky Charms." A petite brunette greeted them with a bright smile and a twinkle in her milk chocolate orbs.

Irish could go for a swim in those eyes. If he hadn't given up his womanizing ways, he'd be all over this beautiful woman, laying on his best charm.

He swallowed his breath as his heart pushed to his throat. Not only was she way out of his league, but he bet she was the kind of lady, one of the rare few, that shot him down in seconds flat.

"Are you looking for some food, or do you want to sit at the bar?" Her voice rolled across his ears like sweet honey on warm bread.

"We're being deployed—"

Irish interrupted Gunny before he could choke out one of the worst lines ever. "A table, please. Thanks."

"Sure thing. Follow me." She turned on her heel and flipped her hair over her shoulder.

Gunny gave him a sideways glance.

Irish shrugged.

She set a couple of menus on the table. "Enjoy your meals, boys."

Irish really wanted to ask her name, but refrained. He wasn't here to pick up some girl and get laid, but he was going to make damn sure that Gunny kept his hands off that one.

Why?

Irish had no fucking clue.

"Are you cock-blocking me for a reason?" Gunny asked with a crooked grin. "Because I told you someone might meet me here."

"She looks familiar," Irish lied. "And I know you. If your friend doesn't show, you'll be on to the next best thing."

"Seriously? You think that little of me."

"I think you're the best," Irish said with an arched brow. "When it comes to having my back. With the ladies, let's face it, neither one of us are relationship material."

"Speak for yourself," Gunny said.

This had never been one of the regular spots that all the men from the base frequented. It's one of the reasons Irish liked it so much. Why he was sharing it with Gunny was a question he couldn't answer.

"I am," Gunny said, twisting the napkin.

"So, you think you and she hooked up years ago?"

"Are we in fucking high school?" It had been a

long time since Irish felt any kind of jealousy and he resented the hell out of the emotion. He had no reason to feel territorial of a woman he didn't even know. And he didn't want to get to know.

Well, that was a lie. Obviously, he had the hots for the pretty hostess, but she was the kind of woman that would rip his heart out.

Just like Jillian.

"Gunny Henderson? As I live and breathe," a female voice screeched from the other side of the room. "I was beginning to think you weren't going to show."

"This is the chick I was telling you about." Gunny smiled and waved. "Hey, good-looking. I'm so glad you could make it." He stood and kissed the cute blond on the cheek. "Daisy, this is a good friend of mine, Irish."

"Oh. That's an interesting name. Is it for real? Or a nickname like Gunny?"

"No. It's my real name and it goes along with my last name, Whiskey." He held out his hand, amused by the way Gunny's eyes lit up like the Fourth of July and how his cheeks turned a little red. "My family has a real odd sense of humor."

"I guess so," Daisy said. "Gunny, I can't believe your stationed at Fort Bragg again."

"I am, but I'm being deployed first thing in the

morning, and it will be a good month before I'm back," Gunny said. "I'm sorry I couldn't have reached out sooner."

"You explained why when we chatted the other day." Daisy planted her hand on her hip and smiled like a wicked sex kitten. "I guess we should get reacquainted then, don't you think?"

"You promise me you haven't been seeing someone," Gunny said. "You know how I feel about that."

"I've been single for the last six months and I think you could use someone to send you letters."

Irish tried real hard not to laugh at the total cheesiness of what was unfolding under his nose. But at the same time, it warmed his heart.

"I need a little more than that," Gunny said. "God, I've missed you."

"I can honestly say the same." Daisy's gaze darted between Gunny and Irish as she bit down on her lower lip.

Irish couldn't help it. He chuckled. "I don't need a babysitter. If you two want to go and *catch up*, I'm a big boy. I can eat all by myself."

"I'll see you in the morning." Gunny was out of his seat in less than two seconds. He and Daisy were out of the restaurant in five flat.

If Irish wasn't so damn hungry, he'd leave.

At least that's what he told himself as he eyed the pretty hostess seating two couples.

He could admire from afar while he enjoyed a medium rare burger, fries, and a seltzer.

It was going to be a long night.

He pulled out his cell and pulled up the app that his family used to text and send insanely cute pictures of all his little second cousins.

Whiskey Fam Bam (Irish): *Hey, all. Just wanted to remind everyone that I'm being deployed tomorrow. As usual. I can't tell you where, but when I have internet, I'll be checking texts, so feel free to send me notes. I always love that.*

He hated to admit how much he missed his family. JW had been right when he said that one day, Irish would think twice about his decision to leave so quickly, but JW hadn't had a drunk for a father or a slut for a mother.

No. JW had a different kind of upbringing, which had been equally as challenging since his parents had died when he'd been a teenager and his uncle, Irish's father, was in no condition to raise his own son, much less four more kids.

The rest of the Whiskey family either lived in Scotland, Ireland, or they just weren't all that close anymore.

Whiskey Fam Bam (JW): *Thanks for letting us know.*

I'm actually sitting here with JD, JB, Georgia Moon, and Luke going over ranch business. An insane amount of pictures of our children coming your way in a few seconds to keep you company. How long will you be gone this time?

Whiskey Fam Bam (Irish): *I honestly don't know, but my guess is three to four weeks based on what I know about the mission.*

Whiskey Fam Bam (JW): *Any chance you have some leave coming up?*

What a loaded question and Irish wasn't willing to tell his cousin, who was more like a brother, the truth.

Not yet.

Whiskey Fam Bam (Irish): *I have some time coming my way and I plan on a trip home. It's been far too long and I need to meet all these rug rats so I can spoil the shit out of them.*

Whiskey Fam Bam (JW): *I'm going to hold you to it.*

He smiled as a slew of images flashed on his screen. The Whiskey family sure knew how to make some damn good-looking kids.

Hopefully, JW would hold to his promise when Irish left fifteen years ago and welcome him back with open arms.

Lorelei Sheldon did her best to keep her gaze from landing on the sexy soldier sitting in the corner booth. However, the second the bouncy blond strutted out the front door with the soldier's buddy, it was all Lorelei could do to keep from going over and checking on the lonely man.

"You're staring." Candice wiped the bar down with a fresh towel as the crowd thinned. "Why don't you just go talk to the guy?"

"Because I don't do military men or anyone that walks through that front door." Lorelei checked her watch. It was close to one in the morning and the bar would be shutting down in an hour.

Hopefully, Mr. Good-looking would be long gone before that.

"Anyone ever tell you that you're going to die a lonely old woman?" Candice said with a sarcastic tone.

"You and Mother every chance you get."

Candice handed her a seltzer. "Bring him a fresh one. On the house."

Lorelei gave the can a once-over. "I would not expect him to be drinking this. Especially mango flavor."

Candice shrugged. "It's all the rage these days. I can't keep the damn stuff stocked." She waved her hand. "Now go. I know he's going to order another one because he ordered onion rings."

"After his burger and fries?" Lorelei asked. "That's impressive."

"And while you're at it, consider yourself clocked out."

Lorelei tilted her head.

"Seriously. It's a light crowd." Candice poured a glass of Lorelei's favorite wine. "Go have a nice conversation. No one says you have to leave with the soldier, but I am, as your boss and best friend, telling you to lighten up and have a good time for a change."

If Lorelei knew nothing else, she knew without a doubt that Candice was not going to let her leave Lucky Charms without bringing a drink over to the corner table, so she might as well get it over with. "Fine." She sucked in a deep breath and let it out slowly, doing her damnedest to clear her mind all while trying to come up with something clever to say.

Like that would ever happen.

By the time she reached the other side of the room, her brain was void of all thoughts.

She cleared her throat. "Hi."

The man looked up. "Hello," he said as he licked his forefinger and thumb. "Is that for me?" He pointed to the seltzer.

"As a matter of fact, it is." She set it on the wood top. "And it's on the house." Nervously, she raised her glass and sipped her wine. The dry crisp pear flavor tingled the inside of her mouth.

"A pity drink for the guy whose buddy ditched him?"

"Oh, God, no. It's not like that at all." She slipped into the booth, setting her glass down and resting her elbows on the table. "My boss sent me over because she thinks I'm pathetic." Shit. That had to be the dumbest thing she'd ever said.

He arched a brow.

"I'm sorry. That didn't come out right."

"No. It didn't." He laughed. "But now I have to know why your boss would believe that about you." He waggled his finger. "After I know who I'm speaking with."

"The name's Lorelei." She stretched out her arm.

"Nice to meet you. I'm Irish. And before you go on about the name. It's not a nickname and the last name is Whiskey."

She covered her mouth to keep from laughing, but it didn't help. "I'm sorry. Sometimes parents don't think before they name."

"Oh. It gets worse." He leaned forward. "One of my cousins is named Jack Daniel's. With the apostrophe and all. And another distant cousin is named

Cosmo. Which isn't a whiskey, but hey. It has Whiskey in the mixings."

"Your family sounds fun."

"They have their moments." He nodded. "Now, I can't imagine that anyone would think you're pathetic. So, please, tell me why your boss pushed you in my direction with a glass of wine."

The real question, at least for Lorelei, was whether or not she should tell the truth or lie. Both could have interesting results and not necessarily in a good way.

"My divorce became final a couple of months ago and Candice, that's my boss and the owner of this place, thinks it's about time I moved on."

"And what do you think?"

She lowered her chin. "That depends on your definition of moving on, because trust me, I'm way over Nico. That's my ex. I'm just not ready to have a man in my life, especially since I went from high school to being married."

"Wow. A teenage bride. How long were you married?"

"Technically, almost ten years. But the last year we were separated and getting divorced, but that always takes time."

"I'm either very sorry, or extremely happy for you."

She laughed. "Thank you. It's actually a little bit of both." She had to appreciate his odd sense of humor, especially when most people cocked their heads and looked at her as though she were about to break, or danced around the subject, making everything awkward and uncomfortable.

"I haven't seen my family in a long time, but we write and text a lot." He waved his cell. "We use some app that one of my cousins set up and when JW first found his ex-fiancée screwing his best friend, he thought his world was about to end, but in the light of day, it was about the best thing that could have happened to him."

"I'm hoping I can think that way soon." She took a long slow slip of her wine. "I've got a foot deeper in the bitter part and haven't quite jumped full force into the sweet end of the pool."

"It takes time and you were married for many years, so it might take a little longer." Irish polished off his last onion ring, wiped his hands, and pushed his plate aside. "Being divorced doesn't make a person pathetic. So, what's the real story with your boss?"

Lorelei wasn't sure if she wanted to answer that. Between half her family, and Candice, Lorelei was pretty tired of the world telling her it was time she experienced *someone else*. But the idea of getting naked in front of anyone other than her husband, or the doctor, made her break out in hives.

It wasn't really the sex the part. She figured that would come naturally and once it started, it would be fine. She knew without a doubt, she could handle that. But it was the intimacy of simply being without clothes in front of another human.

Or sharing a bathroom.

Hell, even brushing her teeth in front of a man wigged her out for some strange reason.

"My ex-husband celebrated our divorce by asking the woman he cheated on me with to marry him and she informed him she was three months pregnant." Wow. Now that wasn't something she planned on saying out loud.

To anyone.

Especially a stranger.

"That sucks."

Oh. He had no idea.

"Do you have kids?"

"No." She shook her head, swallowing the rancid taste that had smacked the back of her throat. "We wanted to have children and it wasn't for lack of trying." She downed the last few gulps of wine. "I actually lost two babies."

"Shit. I'm so sorry."

She let out a short laugh. Talk about pathetic. She

was sitting in a booth, in the middle of the night, telling a perfect stranger her problems. And she wasn't about to stop. Hell. It felt damned good to say these things and not be judged or stared at like she'd done something wrong.

"That must have really been hard on you when you found out about your ex."

She nodded. "I think the worst part, though I didn't know this until after the miscarriage, was that he was cheating when we got pregnant."

"He's a real asshole."

"He certainly turned into one," she said as Candice appeared, slipping half a bottle of wine and another seltzer on the table. Before Lorelei could say anything, Candice was gone. "I would have introduced you, but obviously, Candice didn't give me a chance."

"I take it that's your boss?" he asked.

Lorelei nodded. "She's also the proud owner of this establishment. She took over for her parents about five years ago. And she's my best friend. We go all the way back to preschool."

"That's cool."

"What about you? Married? Serious girlfriend?"

"None of the above," he said. "I've never had the time nor the inclination to settle down and have a family."

She pointed to his phone. "Someone is sending you a ton of baby pictures."

He laughed, picking up his cell. His smile was as wide as the state of Texas. "Those are all my cousins' kids. They always send me a ton right before I'm deployed to keep me company. Cutest little buggers in all the land." He thumbed through a few of them. "They grow so quickly. It seems like just yesterday they all started having kids, but some of them are riding horses and JB's little boy, he's even riding a bull." He turned his cell and held up a picture of a boy about the age of seven on the backside of an angry bucking beast with horns.

"No, thank you." She leaned back, waving her hands. "I've never even been on a horse. I can't imagine riding one of those."

"Yeah. Not my favorite thing to do and I wasn't very good at it either. One of the reasons I left and joined the Army."

"Sounds like you have a great family." Lorelei hoped she didn't come off as a bitter young woman, because she wasn't, or at least she hoped not. Even though it was still hard for her to be around pregnant women and babies, she wanted her friends and family to be happy. She blinked, noticing the distance in Irish's eyes. It wasn't that he seemed sad, but there was an emptiness behind his blue orbs that hadn't been there a few moments ago.

"They are good people and I miss them." He lifted the wine bottle and emptied it into her glass. He chuckled. "For two strangers who just met, we sure did get into a deep conversation."

"That we did." She sipped her wine, feeling the effects and enjoying it a little too much.

"For the record, your ex-husband's a shit for cheating on you."

"I'd have to agree, but I'm divorced and he's someone else's problem now."

"That's the spirit." He clanked his seltzer against her drink. "So, tell me something." He shifted, resting his arm over the back of the bench.

She swallowed the thumping of her heart. No question that started with tell me something and continued with the kind of nervous body language that Irish exhibited ended well.

He rubbed the back of his neck. "Why did you come over here? Because you could have told your friend that you didn't want to."

That wasn't the worst question and not exactly where she thought he was going, but she didn't have an easy answer. "Please don't take this the wrong way, but if I didn't bring you that drink, Candice either would have dragged me kicking and screaming, or she would have made my life a living hell for the next week while still trying to get me to talk to almost any single man that walked through those doors."

"Does Candice believe that you have to be in a relationship to be happy?"

She narrowed her eyes. "Not necessarily."

The corners of his mouth turned upward in a sexy grin. "What exactly was her goal in sending you over here?"

"It doesn't matter. My reason is the only one that counts."

"Fair enough." He nodded as he waved to his waiter. "Well, I have to get up in a few hours and I do believe you probably did enough chatting to keep your friend off your back for a good day or two."

Lorelei laughed. "You're a good sport."

"I have my moments." He took her hand and kissed the backside of it. "It was a pleasure."

"The pleasure was all mine." She leaned back in the booth and tilted her head. Damn, he had a nice ass, and she watched him saunter through the crowd and to the front door.

"You weren't supposed to let him leave alone." Candice appeared, seemingly out of nowhere. She slipped into the booth and glared.

"I'm not having a one-night stand with some

stranger, especially a military man who is being deployed tomorrow. Besides, he wasn't interested."

"And you know this, how?"

"Through casual conversation and body language," she said as she stood. "I'm headed home. I'll see you tomorrow." She turned on her heel and made a beeline for the break room. She'd snag her purse and be out of Lucky Charms in less than five minutes and without listening to another word Candice had to say on the subject of Lorelei's love life.

Or lack thereof.

She didn't need to have a man in her life. What she needed was to figure out what her life looked like without one.

And that's exactly what she intended on doing.

2

_L_orelei pulled her crossbody purse over her shoulder and made her way to the parking lot. While this part of Woodover wasn't a horrible part of town, any place at two in the morning wasn't necessarily safe. She held her keys between her fingers as she scurried across the parking lot of Lucky Charms. Her apartment building was just across the street and around the corner, but on cloudy dark nights like these, she always wished she'd driven.

She glanced to the right and noticed a man with his feet sticking out the window of a Jeep. Her heart lurched to her throat as she clutched her purse tighter. She was about to sprint when she realized it was Irish, and he looked as though he were trying to take a bit of a nap. Inching closer, she made sure her assessment was correct.

"Irish," she whispered.

He lifted his chin and peeked open one eye.

"What the heck are you doing?" she asked.

"I was trying to sleep." He stretched his arms over his head and yawned.

"Why?"

"That last drink put me over the legal limit and I couldn't chance driving."

She reached over the windowsill and snagged the door handle. This had to be one of the worst ideas she'd had since deciding to surprise her husband when deep down, she knew she'd be catching him with his pants down.

And she did it anyway.

She grabbed him by the hand and yanked.

"What the hell do you think you're doing?" He stumbled from the vehicle.

"I'm not going to let you sleep it off in the parking lot of Lucky Charms when I live a block away and have a perfectly good sofa where you can crash for a few hours. Especially when I'm the one who got you drunk."

"For the record, I'm not drunk. Just not safe to drive."

"Same thing," she mumbled, realizing she'd laced her fingers through his, *and* he hadn't stopped her.

"Okay, but I don't think me bunking on your couch is a good idea."

"And why not?" She glanced at him while she waited for the light to change to green. "I don't bite. I promise."

He chuckled. "I'm not worried about you. I, on the other hand, will be tossing and turning and thinking about how I want to do all these inappropriate things to you and I won't get a wink of sleep." He slipped his hand from hers and rested it on the small of her back, nudging her across the street. "While you, on the other hand, will be as snug as a bug in the other room."

Her lips parted and she gasped, unable to respond. She wasn't sure if she was flattered, terrified, or ready to pounce the moment they stepped foot in her apartment. She cleared her throat. "Well, there's only one problem with that scenario."

"Yeah. What's that?"

She stopped in front of her building and turned. "I live in a one-room studio." Ignoring the stunned look on Irish's face, she turned and entered her key code. The door popped open and she stepped into her tiny humble abode, letting Irish decide for himself if he was going to stand outside looking like someone had just told him the most shocking news ever, or come inside and take a load off.

"This is going to be impossible." He pulled the door closed and locked it. "I know I didn't say this before, because it would have sounded like a line and I didn't go into Lucky Charms for anything other than some grub, but I couldn't keep my eyes off you if I tried."

"That's sweet of you to say." She pulled down two glasses from the cabinet. "Water or something stronger?"

"Aqua is perfect, thank you." He leaned against the door and ran a hand across his cleanly buzzed head. "I'm going to apologize for being insanely rude, but if you were my ex-wife, I wouldn't want you—"

She held up her hand. "I don't want his money, so I walked away with nothing and in his defense, he did try to give me something."

"Considering he cheated on you, when you were pregnant with his kid, I would have taken him for every penny."

"Well, I'm not you," she said, biting her tongue. She'd heard it all a million times from family and friends. They all believed she deserved something for her heartache, and maybe she did, but all she really wanted was a clean break and to prove to herself she could make it on her own.

And that meant without Nico's money.

"And I didn't want to be tied to him in any way. He's got his new life and while I don't want to erase our marriage from my memory, I just need to do the things that I never got a chance to because I married him when I was eighteen."

Otherwise, it wasn't truly a fresh start.

"I can understand that." He nodded. "I left home a week after I graduated high school because I wanted to do things my way, not the way of my family. So, I get it." He took the water she handed him, but remained glued to the wall.

Whatever made him happy. She climbed up on the stool by the counter in the so-called kitchen.

"Do you mind if I ask what your ex does for a living?"

"He's a lawyer." She tucked her hair behind her ears. "My parents are still pissed I didn't take what he offered, considering they believe I all but put him through school."

"Did you?"

She shrugged. "He comes from money, so his parents paid for his undergraduate." Pointing to the sofa pushed up under the window, next to her bed, she said, "You might as well make yourself comfortable."

He smiled. "You don't want to know what's going to make me *comfortable*." He waggled his brow.

"You're a flirt."

"I certainly can be and you're not doing a good job at shutting me down." He eased onto her sofa, kicking off his boots and stretching out his long legs. He had to be close to six two. He wasn't overtly muscular, but she suspected under his clothes was a well-defined body that was as hard as a rock. He had a few wrinkles around his bright-blue eyes. If he was a day over thirty-three, she'd be shocked, and she was really good at guessing ages.

The question she had to ask herself, and she needed to be honest, was if she wanted to let things happen naturally, or if she wanted to stop things dead in their tracks right now. The more she allowed her mind to mentally undress the man staring at her with sex dripping from his gaze, the more she realized her desires outweighed all her fears and insecurities.

What the hell.

She'd probably never see him again, and if she read him correctly, that's exactly what he wanted as well.

"And what if I don't want to shut you down?"

He coughed. "A year ago, I'd be jumping off this couch and wrapping my arms around you, kissing you softly, tenderly, making my best moves, and not worrying about the consequences."

"And what's changed?"

"While I'm not looking for a relationship, because I don't want that, at all, I'm tired of using women for a single night of fun."

"Who says you're using me?"

He stood, sauntering his way across the room, which took all of ten steps. "You're making this impossible for me to be a gentleman."

She dropped her hands over his shoulders, pressing her lips on his warm cheek. In all her life, she'd never had a one-night stand. Hell, she'd never had sex with anyone other than Nico and as far as kissing or heavy petting? That had only happened two other times, both ending incredibly awkwardly, and she'd prefer not to think about either time. "Something tells me that no matter the situation, you're always gentlemanly."

"My grandmother, may she rest in peace, would have loved to hear you say that, but trust me when I say, I've been trying to turn over a new leaf, and you're making it impossible for me to change my stripes."

She pressed her chest against his and inhaled

sharply. "What kind of a man do you think you used to be?"

"A love 'em and leave 'em type." He curled his thick fingers around her hips.

Her nipples tightened. Heat spread across her skin and through her veins. At one point she'd loved her husband. Worshipped the ground Nico had walked on and all she'd wanted to do was please him, both in and out of bed.

At one time, he made her feel like she was the most desirable woman in the world.

However, never in her life had she ever taken on the role of huntress, and boy, was she on the prowl and had no intention of letting Irish leave.

Not without pulling out all the stops.

"And what if that is exactly what I need right now?"

"No one *needs* to be treated the way I've been treating ladies my entire adult life. Not even someone who isn't looking for romance or a long-term thing." He took her chin with his thumb and forefinger. "I'm not a nice man."

She smiled. Her heart swelled. "Only a kind, caring person would say that." Taking a risk, she brushed her lips over his, slipping her tongue into his hot mouth.

He groaned, pulling her closer. His lids fluttered

over his smoldering eyes as he deepened the kiss, making it more passionate and filling her body with a kind of primal hunger she'd only read about in books. "You have to know that you will never see me again because I'm not coming back."

"What do you mean?"

"No one in my circle of friends knows this, but I'm not re-enlisting. Once this mission is done, I'll be heading out back west never to look back on this part of my life."

"Please don't take this the wrong way, but that's exactly what I want." She splayed her hand across the center of his chest, toying with his tender skin. "I've only known one man. Everyone keeps telling me I need to get back in the saddle, but I'm not ready for dating or relationships. And having a one-night stand with someone you might run into on a regular basis, well, that could be—"

He pressed his finger against her lips. "Meaningless sex is overrated."

"It wouldn't be totally senseless and without purpose." She took a step back and raised her shirt over her head, showing off her lacy black bra.

His gaze lowered as his hands roamed across her bare stomach.

"Do you want me?" she asked with a shaky voice.

"Very much so." He leaned in and kissed the top

swell of her breasts. "That's not even close to the issue." He palmed her cheek. "When I walk out that door, I won't be back, and I don't want you to regret inviting me in."

She opened her mouth, but he hushed her with a quick, but powerful kiss.

"You had expectations for a certain kind of life and I believe you still want it. Sleeping with a bad boy isn't going to change that."

"I never said it would." She unhooked her under-garment and let it fall to her feet. The last person, other than her doctor to see her this vulnerable, hadn't appreciated her.

By the wide eyes and jaw-dropping gape, she'd guess that Irish more than enjoyed what he saw.

"I'm not asking you for anything other than a good time and a little respect when you leave."

He tore off his T-shirt and began working on the zipper to his jeans. "Respecting you will be the easy part," he said. "The rest of it, well, you've put a big burden on my shoulders. I'm a little nervous I won't—"

"I sincerely doubt you're scared about perform-ing." She looped her finger into his pants, helping him tug them over his hips. Her heart hammered in her throat. Never in a million years had she expected to be standing in the middle of her studio apartment,

31

half naked, helping a man, who wasn't her husband, take his clothes off.

And not only was she enjoying it, but she wasn't embarrassed by it one little bit.

As a matter of fact, she was empowered by the entire experience.

She removed the rest of his clothes, as well as her own before tumbling onto her bed in his arms, laughing, which wasn't something she'd ever done while making love before.

Her ex-husband was always way too serious in bed. She used to tease him that he needed to leave the courtroom at the office. Nico didn't find that amusing at all, especially since he worked twenty hours a day.

"You need a new box spring." Irish cupped one breast, pinching and twisting the nipple while he took the other one into his mouth. His tongue swirled over the top, making it tingle.

She arched her back, moaning, begging for more.

And more he gave to the point she couldn't catch her breath. She gasped for air, but couldn't fill her lungs no matter how hard she tried.

He dotted little kisses down her stomach to her belly button. His fingers found her hard nub and rubbed gentle circles.

Digging her heels into the mattress, she lifted her

head, staring down at him as he kissed her intimately. She'd never watched a man do this to her before and she couldn't turn away, even if she wanted to.

In the past, she'd always close her eyes tight and focus on the sensations, which she loved, but she didn't have a desire to view the intimate act.

Until now.

He glanced up while slipping his fingers inside, gliding gently, but with purpose. He smiled just as he flicked his tongue.

"Oh, God," she said with a throaty moan.

"You're so close," he said. "I want to be inside you."

"Yes. Yes." She wiggled underneath him as he adjusted his body.

"I didn't think this through," he whispered. "I don't have a condom."

"I have one in the nightstand." She cupped his face. "Candice wanted me to be prepared just in case."

He chuckled. "Well, you'll have to thank her for me sometime." He reached across her body and found the foil package and ripped it open. After covering himself, he nuzzled his head between her legs again, bringing her to the point of no return.

It took only a couple of minutes, maybe less,

before she was begging him to bring her over the edge. It amazed her how quickly he'd learned everything about her body and what she liked. What made her erogenous zones light up like there was no tomorrow.

"Please. Now, Irish."

"How about you be in control." He rolled to his back, tossing her leg over his thigh. He gripped her hips as his chest rose up and down with each choppy breath.

She rocked back and forth. His fingers dug into her skin. With every move, his muscles flexed. He groaned, biting down on his lower lip. His lids grew heavy over his smoldering eyes. Grinding her hips, she moved harder and faster. Her toes curled and she leaned forward, curling her fingers around his shoulders.

His hips thrust up to meet her every motion until her inside exploded over him and he pulled her close to his chest.

"Yes, Lorelei," he whispered. "Lose control."

She loved how her name glided off his tongue like warm butter melting into all the nooks and crannies of a waffle.

Shuddering, she collapsed on top of him as her climax tore through her bloodstream. Her lungs burned as she tried to fill them.

His hands ran up and down her back and gently threaded through her hair while he whispered such sweet, kind words in her ear.

She kissed his neck. "Thank you."

"For what?" He cocked his head back, cupping her face, staring into her eyes, searching for some kind of answer.

"For the orgasm of the century?"

He burst out laughing as he pulled the covers over their bodies. "I have to say it was the best one I've had in forever."

"You're just saying that."

He kissed her nose. "Actually, I'm not." He closed his eyes, letting out a slow breath. "If I were any other man and you weren't trying to figure out who you are on your own, I'd be asking if we could do this again."

"When do you have to leave?"

He glanced at his watch. "Two hours, so if I can have at least an hour and fifteen of shut-eye, I might be able to give a repeat performance."

"I'll set the alarm." With more enthusiasm than was necessary, she found her cell. She glanced at Irish and her heart sunk to her gut when she saw his shocked expression. "Oh, God. You were joking, weren't you?"

He shook his head. "I just didn't expect you to

take me up on the offer." He tucked her head onto his chest and kissed her forehead. "Now, we should at least try to sleep for a bit."

She would try, but her mind wouldn't shut down.

Nor would her body.

And she suspected that for the rest of her life, this would be the sexual experience with which she measured all others.

*T*rish knew he'd made a big mistake when he snapped a picture of Lorelei cooking breakfast.

However, the bigger issue was his refusal to delete the damn thing.

He ran his thumb over the picture as he sat in the debriefing room. He'd never met anyone who had such grace and beauty as Lorelei. Her ex-husband was a moron for letting her go.

A warm shiver coated his skin. The last time he'd felt like this he'd ended up having his heart ripped to shreds in a matter of two months. He'd fallen hard and fast for Jillian and he'd foolishly thought she felt the same way.

But the second the shit got real, she was out the door and she didn't look back.

Since then, Irish protected not just his heart, but his soul. And Lorelei was the kind of woman who he'd give both to without thinking twice.

He really needed to make sure he was always thinking, which was why he left without exchanging any phone numbers. He couldn't afford to become entangled with anyone.

Not right now.

"Good morning." Gunny slapped him on the back.

Irish jumped. "Jesus. You scared me." He tapped his phone and set it screen down. Snagging his water bottle, he twisted the cap and took a big gulp. Not only did Gunny sneak up on him, but Irish had been reliving the one thing that had wigged him out during the course of the night.

The broken condom.

She had explained to him about how long it took for her to get pregnant and how she had to take fertility drugs and the likelihood she could ever get pregnant on her own without medical help was slim to none had calmed his nerves. He believed her. And the fact she let him walk out of her life without a phone number spoke volumes to her character. If she were trying to trap him somehow, she would have been begging him for his cell—just in case.

But she didn't do that.

And she had no idea where he was from, or where he was going.

But still. What if she had gotten pregnant? What then?

He'd already had one woman do the unspeakable. He could reach out when he returned.

"Sorry. It's not like I didn't just see you five minutes ago." Gunny took a seat across the table and fiddled with his half-empty cup of coffee. "You've been way too serious about this mission."

Their commander had gone over the mission, which had taken up almost six hours. It wasn't going to be an easy one. As a matter of fact, it was probably one of the most difficult and dangerous jobs Irish had ever seen laid out on paper. He and his team would be lucky to make it out alive.

Of course, that was true of many missions, but this one was a little trickier than the last one since they were going in as an unsanctioned mission if it failed, sanctioned if they were successful.

That always sucked.

Nothing like going out with a bang.

"I was just thinking about my family. I got a whole bunch of pictures of all my little cousins last night and this morning. They are growing like wildfire."

"Kids do that," Gunny said. "Thanks for being so

cool about me leaving last night. Daisy is something special and if I were ever in one spot, I'd really think twice about my single status."

"Do you want to know what I think?"

"No. But you're going to tell me anyway."

Irish chuckled. "You've been in love with this Daisy girl for some time now and I'd gather a wager that she's pretty smitten with you."

"Love is a pretty strong word," Gunny said, but he couldn't wipe the smile off his face. "Where did everyone go?"

Irish shrugged. "Calling their families, wives, kids, one last time before we hop on that transport plane."

"You've been very melancholy all morning. What's going on with you?" Leave it to Gunny to pick up on Irish's emotions.

The worst part was that Irish was known for his cool demeanor and he never wore his feelings on his sleeve. As a matter of fact, everyone on his team often asked if his heart was made out of stone. Not that he didn't care about his brothers-in-arms, that went without saying, but when it came to members of the opposite sex, he kept his emotions to himself.

"I haven't told anyone on the team yet, though our commander knows."

"Now you're scaring me." Gunny set his coffee down and leaned forward. "Talk to me, man."

"You can't tell anyone."

Gunny nodded.

"This is my last deployment. I didn't re-enlist and my last day in the Army is five weeks away."

"Holy fuck." Gunny wiped his brow. "Why didn't you tell anyone?"

"I don't know. I didn't want to make a big deal about it and I'd rather the rest of the guys not know until we get back."

Gunny nodded. "I can respect that. I just can't believe you're leaving the Army. What made you decide that?"

Irish wasn't even sure anymore what had been the driving force, other than he wasn't satisfied with his life or career choice. Every deployment left him with an empty sensation in the center of his gut and a hole in his heart. He just had no idea what he wanted to do after the military, and it wasn't ranching; that was for damn sure. "I wish I understood where the restlessness came from," Irish admitted. If there was anyone he could talk to, it would be Gunny. "I just know I need a change."

"You could have asked for a transfer."

"Now you sound like our commander." Irish let

out a long breath. "Trust me when I say I've been thinking about this for a while."

"Are you going to go back to Buhl, Idaho?"

"I might go for a visit, but not to stay. I'm not sure ranching is for me either."

"Well, how the hell would you know? You left home when you were barely eighteen."

An image of Lorelei in her pajama bottoms and tank top dancing around the kitchen while she made him a bagel and a cup of coffee to go popped into his mind. She had a young free spirit that tickled Irish's heart in a way that no woman ever had.

Of course, he never let anyone in and the ladies he dated were emotionally unavailable. He generally dated professional women who were eager to climb the corporate ladder and didn't have time for a man in their lives. Not that Lorelei wanted a relationship, which she made clear, but that all of a sudden became the biggest turn-on and right about now, Irish wished they had exchanged contact information.

But then what?

He had no idea what to do with his life, so how could he ask a woman to become romantically involved with him when he couldn't even imagine what that would look like?

"I guess I don't," Irish admitted. "I just know I

need some time and space to myself and think things through."

"I'm here if you need a sounding board, anytime."

"I appreciate that, man."

"What are the brothers you choose for?" Gunny smiled. "Besides, you're going to have to keep me sane the next few weeks. You might have been right about that love stuff. I think I've had it bad for Daisy for years; I just haven't wanted to admit it to myself."

The rest of the team filed back into the room. Irish took the opportunity to steal one last look at Lorelei before safely tucking her picture in a folder, where his buddies wouldn't accidentally find it. Not that anyone looked at his phone, he just thought it would be good to make it hard to find.

Even for himself.

Besides, he needed to forget about the sexy hostess. He had too many life issues to figure out, as did she.

It was time to step out of his comfort zone and into...he had no idea.

Lorelei found herself glancing at the front door of Lucky Charms every time it opened, hoping Irish would step into the restaurant, but knowing he wouldn't.

"I can't believe you let him leave without you last night." Candice wiped down the bar area, setting two glasses of water in front of two regulars who were waiting for a couple of burgers and fries. "He was hot for you."

If Lorelei told Candice the truth, she'd want the details, which would make Lorelei blush.

She touched her cheeks, feeling the heat rise.

"Oh, my God. You met up with him, didn't you?" Candice grabbed her by the forearm. "Tony, you've got the bar, and Ellen, you've got the hostess station." She dragged Lorelei through the back room and into her office where she opened her mini fridge and pulled out a bottle of white and poured two glasses. "Start talking, girlfriend."

"There isn't anything to say because I won't ever see him again."

"Are you fucking kidding me?" Candice took a long sip. "You did sleep with him, right?"

"That's none of your business." Lorelei downed half the glass of wine, without even tasting it. She had no idea if it was an oaked chardonnay or sweet Pinot Gris and she didn't care.

"Well, I'll be damned. I bet he was good in bed."

"Do you hear yourself?" Lorelei rubbed her

temples. As if she expected Candice to be less up front. "Can you be any less crude?"

"I'm sorry. It's just that you've done nothing but act like your life was over ever since you and Nico split up."

"That's because all my hopes and dreams ended when I lost that baby and Nico and his new bride got pregnant." Lorelei hadn't meant to sound so bitter, but she still resented how cruel life's twists and turns had ruined her well-laid plans. She and Nico had wanted a family. He still did, just not with her, and that hurt more than she cared to admit.

She flattened her hand over her stomach. Last night she and Irish had made love three times. She had no idea that was even possible, and she felt bad that he hadn't slept a single minute.

And then there was the broken condom, to which she wasn't overly concerned about. She had to talk him off the ledge, telling him her life story about self-injections and the miscarriages, and her angry uterus. The chances of her ever giving birth was about the same as Irish going to the moon.

A harsh reality that she'd finally come to terms with the day her divorce had become final and her ex told her he was going to be a father.

Fucking asshole.

"Oh, honey. I know Nico hurt you in the worst

way. But please know that you're better off without him now."

Lorelei nodded. "It's taken me some time, but I do get that." She made herself comfortable in the small love seat that Candice kept in the corner of her office.

Candice tucked her feet under her butt. "So, did you have fun last night?"

Lorelei couldn't contain her smile. "It was the most amazing night of my life. Better than anything I can remember."

"Are you going to see him again?"

Lorelei shook his head. "We didn't exchange information." She held up her hand. "He's got his own problems and he's only here temporarily. And trust me, I'm okay with this." Her body warmed as she remembered every gentle kiss of his lips. "It was a magical moment that I will cherish. But that's all it was."

"Well, then I'm glad you had it."

"Thanks for pushing me," Lorelei said. "But don't do it again. Once was enough. Got it?"

"Understood." Candice nodded. "Now, I think we both better get back to work."

Lorelei set her drink down on the desk before hugging her best friend and making her way back out to the main floor where she came face-to-face with the young woman who had left with Irish's buddy. "Oh. Hello," she said. "Can I get you a table?"

"That would be lovely. One in the corner, if you don't mind?"

"Sure thing." Lorelei grabbed a menu. "Are you meeting anyone?"

"I wish," the woman said. "I think I officially have a boyfriend now, but he was deployed today and I just want to have his favorite meal in his honor while writing him a long email."

Lorelei nodded. "Gunny, right?"

"Yes. Do you know him well?"

"No. But I'm friendly with his buddy, Irish."

"Ah. The man Gunny was with last night. Are you his girlfriend or something?"

"No. Just a friend," Lorelei said. "What's your name?"

"Daisy."

"Well, Daisy. Follow me. I've got a perfect table for you and if you need anything, I'm Lorelei. Just ask." It probably wasn't the brightest thing in the world for her to become friendly with Daisy, especially when the idea was never to see, hear from, or have any contact with Irish ever again.

But this made Lorelei feel as though she hadn't ripped the Band-Aid off so harshly.

4

THREE WEEKS LATER...

*L*orelei blew out a puff of air and stared at the word *pregnant* on the stick. It couldn't be possible. She'd spent three years trying to get pregnant the first time and two years the second time.

How the hell could she get knocked up in one night?

That didn't happen.

At least not to her.

Gently, she placed the stick in a plastic bag and put it back in her purse. As if she waited long enough the answer would change.

She smoothed down the front of her slacks and stepped from the bathroom at Lucky Charms. It was a slow night for a Thursday, which didn't help to keep her mind occupied with thoughts other than

Irish and his baby.

A baby.

What the fuck was she going to do?

Her gaze shifted to the main door. She gasped as Daisy entered with her arm draped over Gunny. Lorelei swallowed her beating heart. If Gunny had returned back to Fort Bragg, then that meant Irish could be in town, depending on when he got his walking papers.

"Hi, Daisy." Lorelei tucked two menus under her arm. "You're all smiles tonight."

"Do you remember Gunny?" Daisy tilted her head, leaning into his body.

"I do. It's good to see you again."

"You as well," Gunny said.

"Shall I show you to a table in the corner where you can have a little privacy and where it's a bit quiet?" Lorelei asked.

"That would be greatly appreciated." Gunny laced his fingers through Daisy's. It was a sweet gesture and Lorelei was genuinely happy for the couple.

"If you don't mind me asking, how long have you been back from your mission?" Lorelei asked. "Your buddy, Irish, told me about it," she added, not wanting him to think that Daisy went around blabbing about her potential new boyfriend, since Daisy had mentioned she was worried he might not feel as strongly as she did.

Gunny arched a brow. "You know Irish?"

"Not really. Just in passing." She turned and navigated her way through the thin crowd, finding a nice booth in the back room. She set the menus on the wood top and stepped aside. "Although, if you wouldn't mind passing along a message for me."

"Sure," Gunny said. "Though he's only in town for about a week and he's a got a shit ton to do in that short time."

"I'm sure." She tucked her hands in her back pockets to keep them from shaking. "Would you ask him if he could stop by before he leaves town? I need to talk to him about something."

Gunny nodded. "I'll give him the message."

"Thanks. I appreciate it." Now all she had to do was wait for the man to show up.

She glanced over her shoulder. Gunny had leaned across the table, taking both of Daisy's hands.

Way too stinking cute.

Lorelei's stomach rolled over. She flattened a hand on her tummy, trying to settle the acid down as it lurched to the back of her throat. She'd promised not only herself, but Irish, that she had no desire to try to contact him after their one night. That she didn't need anything from him.

And she didn't.

If there was one thing she knew for sure, it was the fact she could raise this baby on her own. And she'd do just that.

However, she owed it to her child to inform its father of its existence. She expected absolutely nothing from Irish. He could be involved if he wanted to, or he could walk away, guilt free.

That was his call, but she couldn't live with herself if she didn't give him that choice.

Irish tossed his rucksack in the back seat of his Jeep. It was about a thirty-six-hour drive back to Buhl, Idaho, but he planned on taking his sweet time. He told his family to expect him in a week. That would give him some time to think about what he wanted to do in this next chapter of his life and the good news was that he did have some job offers on the table.

Two of which weren't ranching.

Both of those jobs were working for ex-military guys who opened their own bodyguard or private investigating firms and that was something Irish could get on board with.

"I can't believe you're leaving." Gunny pushed his

sunglasses up on his head. "We've been through a lot together, you and me."

"That we have." Irish nodded.

"It's going to suck being stationed at Fort Bragg alone."

Irish laughed. "But you have Daisy." For a few years, all he'd heard from Gunny was little tidbits about this girl Daisy. It was obvious to everyone that Gunny was madly in love with her; he just hadn't figured it out yet and there was this little problem of geography.

Something that Irish understood because it was a big problem with Jillian in the sense she wouldn't even consider moving when he was transferred.

Gunny smiled and if Irish wasn't mistaken, his cheeks turned slightly red. Irish had nothing against love, marriage, and family. It just wasn't for him, and when anyone asked, he could give a dozen valid reasons why.

And it wasn't just because his mother had run off with another man or his father had been a shit and drank himself to death. Nor was he afraid of being a father, like he'd be a terrible one or something, like most people accused him.

He knew he was a decent man with a kind heart.

So, that argument was bullshit.

For years, it was his career that he used for his

reasons that family life wasn't in the cards. Well, he no longer had that ace up his sleeve and since he was only thirty-three, age wasn't a factor. However, he was in no frame of mind to be giving his heart, mind, and soul to a woman, or a child. Not until he straightened out in his head how his life had gotten so derailed.

Actually, he knew the moment things had changed in his world. It was the day Jillian had told him she had taken care of *it*.

He hadn't even known *it* existed. He understood it was her body and her right. But she'd been pregnant with *his* kid. He had a right to know, and he certainly deserved a conversation. It didn't matter that they'd broken up because she wouldn't move with him and she didn't love him.

He almost laughed at himself because for all the women he'd used for sex, Jillian had done the same to him, only she lied to him about her feelings. She told him she was falling in love with him when he shared how much he cared and how he'd never felt that way before.

He gave into his vulnerabilities and she was just looking for a good time.

All she had to do was tell him that and he would have given that to her once or twice, and then he would have moved on, with his heart intact.

And he would have never known what it felt like to have been told he was going to be a father.

And seconds later have it taken away.

"It's strange to go from playing the field for all of my adult life to being in an exclusive relationship that also feels like we've been together forever."

"Well, you did mention that you've had an on again off again thing with her for years, so that helps."

Gunny nodded. "She's something special."

Irish squeezed his buddy's shoulder. "So are you and I'm going to miss you. Promise me that when you get the chance, you'll come out and see me, wherever I land."

"You bet," Gunny said. "So, I have to ask. What did the hostess at Lucky Charms want?"

Shit. Irish was hoping to avoid that question. "I honestly don't know. I haven't had the chance to stop by." He reached for his back pocket and felt the envelope with the handwritten note. It was the best he could do because if he stopped to see Lorelei, he might not ever leave, and he had to go and do some serious soul-searching. Something he desperately needed to do.

"Did something happen between the two of you?"

It was rare that Gunny ever interjected himself into Irish's love life, mostly because Irish never had one, except for Jillian, and Gunny knew better than to bring her up. But either Daisy had said something, or Gunny had picked up on Irish's emotions.

Anything was possible at this point.

"Something would have if I stayed, I think."

"She seems like a real nice lady."

Irish nodded. A different time. A different place. He and Lorelei might have had a running chance. Well, he'd have to be a completely different man, but again, anything was possible. "I better hit the road. When you see Lorelei tell her I'm sorry I didn't get a chance to say goodbye." He wished he wasn't such a coward, but he couldn't face her in fear of begging her to take a road trip with him, or worse.

He wouldn't leave.

Her memory got him through some long nights on his last mission, something that he'd never be able to repay her for.

Irish pulled Gunny in for a bro hug, slapping him on the back before slipping behind the steering wheel. He pressed the button and revved the engine. Waving, he hit the gas and pulled out into traffic, not looking back, because if he did, he might actually get teary-eyed.

It took him eight minutes to get from the front of the base to Lorelei's apartment. He'd already checked and she was working, which is why he decided to leave in the early afternoon. That way he could drop the note at her door and be on his way.

Again, he called himself a coward.

But at least he left her a note. It was better than blowing her off altogether.

That was the bill of goods he was selling himself.

5

*L*orelei blinked. The bright sun stung her eyes, even with her darkest shades on. She leaned against the door and stared at the vast mountain ranges and the wide-open spaces of Idaho. She'd never seen anything like it before in her entire life. Growing up in North Carolina, she believed she had the best of all worlds.

She had the mountains. Lakes. And the ocean all nearby.

But nothing could have prepared her for the inherent beauty of Buhl, Idaho.

It took her breath away.

"We'll be at the ranch in five minutes," the driver of the car service said. "Are you there for the riding school?"

"No," she said.

"It's a huge place. Do you know where on the ranch you want me to drop you?"

Shit. She hadn't thought this through. "The main residence."

The driver glanced in the rearview mirror. "There's more than one, ma'am."

Just one more thing she didn't know. She glanced at her watch. It was three in the afternoon on a Tuesday. Whiskey Ranch was a business. "How about the main administrative building."

"That I can do."

"Thanks." She pulled out the letter Irish left her and opened it. She still wasn't sure how she felt about the words on the page.

Or the man who wrote them.

Dear Lorelei,

I don't even know where to begin, except for to say thank you. This last mission was a difficult one. We lost two good men. Not on my team, but still, I knew them and one of them had just had his first kid. A little girl named Delilah. I have no idea why I just told you that because it has nothing to do with anything other than our night together helped me get through many rough evenings.

You're a special lady. I mean that. And I don't say that to many people.

Hell, I don't think I've ever written a letter like this.

I know. I should have stopped by, especially when you asked me to, but I have to assume that if it were really important, you would have hunted me down.

I have no valid reason for not coming, except for to say I have a lot going on. Or maybe I have nothing going on, but it's all life changes and I don't know which end is up.

And I meant what I said. I can't give you anything and I didn't want to hurt you. I truly hope I haven't. I don't regret our night and I hope you don't either. Please understand that when I walked out that morning I couldn't ever look back or come back. This part of my life is over and it's time I go find out who I am now.

Maybe if we met in a different time or different place we could have seen if there was more. I don't know. Call me crazy. I do feel a connection to you and that's why I felt I owed you an explanation. I'm sorry if it's not a good enough one.

I wish you well and I will always think of you fondly.
Your friend,
Irish Whiskey
Whiskey Ranch, Buhl, Idaho

She folded the letter as the dark SUV drove through a large gate with a sign that read Whiskey Ranch. She found it interesting that he signed the letter with the name of the family ranch.

That had to mean something.

She hoped.

Her heart hammered in her chest so fast she thought it was going to jump right out of her chest. Irish had left North Carolina three days ago. She had no idea if he'd made it this far yet or not. She could have called, but based on this note, he would have blown her off.

And she couldn't have that.

Her news was too big and she couldn't tell him over the phone.

This had to be done face-to-face.

She sucked in a deep breath and counted to ten, letting it out slowly as the vehicle rolled to a stop in front of an old farmhouse turned into an office building.

"Would you like me to wait or anything?" the driver asked.

"I think I'll be okay." She snagged her backpack and small suitcase. "Thanks again."

"Anytime. You have my card. If something changes in the next half hour, I can turn around and come get you."

She stepped out into the cool summer air. It was much dryer than in the Carolinas and she liked the way it felt against her skin. She climbed up the eight steps and set her roller bag on the porch. She glanced around and smiled as someone on a horse rode by. This was right out of a made-for-television show and she loved every second of it.

Only, the second she turned and faced the door, all the butterflies came back. She gathered all the courage she could and stepped inside.

"May I help you?" a young woman asked. She wore a pair of jeans, a white tank top, and carried one kid on her hip while holding the hand of a small boy, maybe about the age of seven.

"Um. Yes. I'm looking for Irish Whiskey." Lorelei adjusted her backpack, gripping the strap as if it were some kind of lifeline.

The woman's eyes grew wide. "Irish isn't here."

Lorelei's stomach turned over. She'd practiced what she would say a million times, but currently she couldn't find a single word. She cleared her throat. "When do you expect him?"

The woman tilted her head. "May I ask who you are and what you want with Irish?"

"My name's Lorelei Sheldon and my business with Irish is personal."

"I see. I'm Cheyenne Whiskey. Can you give me a second?"

"Sure." Lorelei assumed Cheyenne must be one of the owners and definitely related to Irish, but perhaps by marriage based on the first name. He did say most of his family were named after whiskey and drinks.

Cheyenne scurried off between a few desks and into the back of the main room. She disappeared into an office with her little boy constantly glancing over his shoulder with a puzzled expression.

Lorelei stood awkwardly in the front of the building, trying not to stare at the staff sitting behind their desks in their cubicles, wondering what the hell they were doing. This was a ranch, not a bank. Where were all the sexy ranch hands and cowboys?

Oh. She shifted her weight as two very handsome men wearing jeans, with large belt buckles, boots, dark T-shirts, and cowboy hats strutted across the room. One of them had the young boy on his back.

"Lorelei. This is my husband, JB Whiskey, and his brother JD."

"Why don't we step outside." JB set the boy down, giving him a fist pound before kissing his wife's cheek.

"Did something happen to Irish?" A brick dropped to the bottom of her stomach. Driving across country anything could happen.

"No. Nothing like that," JD said as he stepped

outside. "Why don't you have a seat." He waved to the chairs on the front porch.

"I've got to get the kids off to the school. I'll catch up to you later," Cheyenne said. "It was nice meeting you."

"Likewise," Lorelei said.

Both JD and JB made themselves comfortable on the long bench.

Lorelei opted for a single chair. She set her backpack on the wood floor and sat up tall. She had no idea what to expect, but she didn't think it was going to be good. She made sure to breathe through her nose. Slow and controlled. "I just need to know when Irish is going to get here. I don't mean to take up any of your time."

"That's the problem; we don't know when he plans on arriving at the ranch," JD said.

"All we know is that he's coming," JB added.

She took a strand of hair and twisted it between her fingers. She hadn't done that since she asked her husband for a divorce. "I was under the impression he'd be here this week."

JB leaned forward. He took his cowboy hat off and rested it on his knee. "He called us yesterday and said he was taking his time."

"He said he wanted to see the countryside," JD

said. "He's been all over the globe with the Army, but he's barely seen the United States."

Lorelei's eyes burned. She stood and turned. Gripping the railing, she stared out over the vast ranch. In the distance, she could see a corral with horses. Some were being walked and others were being ridden. She sucked in a deep breath. The fresh air filled her lungs. It smelled like a combination of honey and pine. "I need to talk to him."

"Why don't you call him?" JD asked.

"This can't be done over the phone. Besides, I don't have his number," she whispered. She knew she shouldn't allow herself to be so vulnerable in front of his cousins. They could be thinking any number of things with a strange woman chasing Irish down.

"Do you want us to call him and tell him you're here?" JD asked.

She blew out a puff of air. "I guess so."

The floorboards rattled under her feet. She blinked as JB leaned against the railing. He ran a hand through his shoulder-length hair. "I don't mean to pry into your personal business. However, I suspect what you have to tell him is something my wife didn't tell me for nearly four years."

She snapped her gaze in his direction. "Excuse

me?" She blinked, unable to completely wrap her brain around his words. "What does that mean?"

"You met Cheyenne and my two kids, Jimmy and Ella, only I didn't know about Jimmy until he was four years old."

"Shit. I'm sorry. That had to have been hard for you," she said.

"Long story short, my wife was engaged to another man when we met. They divorced because he knew Jimmy wasn't his kid, but when Cheyenne left me, I made it pretty clear we were done, so she didn't feel like she could come to me. I ran into her at a rodeo, and the second I saw Jimmy, I knew. Ironically, she was on her way to tell me about him."

"But that's four years you missed out on."

JB nodded. "Forgiveness is easy when you understand all the circumstances, and we're together now. And happy. That's all that matters."

"Why are you telling me this?" Lorelei asked.

"I want to know how much I need to push Irish to get his ass back to this ranch," JB said.

"We know this is personal," JD interjected. "And none of our business, but Irish is going through something. We don't know what it is, but the Army was the only thing that had given meaning to his life. And now, he's a lost, wounded soul wandering the countryside."

"JW, our oldest brother, first thought Irish was being an idiot for leaving," JB said. "But we all went to his graduation from boot camp and we all saw that the Army was exactly where Irish belonged. So, when he called and said he was retiring long before he got all his time in, we were shocked."

"Not to mention he didn't seem to be himself."

"I don't know Irish very well," she admitted, still twirling her hair. Her nerves burned her skin starting at her toes and crawling up to the top of her head. "But what little time I did spend with him, he did appear a little lost and lonely." She closed her eyes for a few seconds. "I feel like I'm betraying his trust even though he didn't tell me not to say anything nor did he reveal any great truths about himself."

JB reached out and gently squeezed her shoulder. "We don't know what happened to Irish. But about a year ago, he called my sister, Georgia Moon. He was upset about something. He was drunk, so he was hard to understand, but the next day, he called back and apologized and said he'd just gotten back from a rough mission. However, since then, he's been different."

"I didn't know him a year ago." Lorelei rubbed the back of her neck. "I know his last mission was tough. He said a few good men died."

"That unfortunately happens in his line of work." JD took out a toothpick from his front pocket and plopped it in his mouth. "To be honest, I don't think it's that because JW called his best friend, Gunny, and they hadn't been on a mission in five weeks when Irish had called my sister. Gunny knows what happened, but he won't give us the details. He said that's up to Irish."

"Gunny's a good friend to Irish," Lorelei said.

"He's the best." JB nodded. "But Irish isn't just our cousin. He's another brother to us. And because of what happened between me and Cheyenne, I know a little more about what happened to Irish than my family does."

"You do?" JD adjusted his cowboy hat. "How is that possible?"

"Irish told me when I called to tell him I had a kid." JB held up his hand. "Irish shared a story with me and he swore me to secrecy and I think that tale is important to what you have to tell him."

"I'm totally confused," JD said.

"So am I," Lorelei admitted. "I just need to talk to Irish. If you point me in the direction of an inexpensive hotel that's close by, I can wait until he gets here."

"You can stay here on the ranch," JB said. "We have plenty of room."

"I don't want to be a bother." But she was also on a budget, so she should just say yes and be done with it.

"It's no problem," JB said. "We can put you up in the cabin that Irish will be staying in when he gets here. It's got two bedrooms and you'd have your privacy."

"Thank you. I really appreciate it. I promise, as soon as Irish and I get to talk, I'll be out of your way."

"I'll go call Irish and tell him you're here." JD took two steps toward the door.

"Maybe that's not the best idea." JB pushed from the railing. "When he called Georgia Moon, it was because he was heartbroken over a woman."

"Irish?" JD asked with a high-pitched voice. "Our cousin, the confirmed bachelor, had his heart crushed?"

"He did. But it had less to do with the girl and more to do with her actions." JB ran a hand through his wavy hair. "He's going to kill me for telling you all this, but he'd fallen in love with this woman who turned out didn't return his feelings. She ended up pregnant and—"

Lorelei gasped, clutching her middle. "What happened to the baby?"

"She had an abortion, but she didn't tell Irish

until after she'd done it," JB said. "He hasn't been the same since."

"Yeah. That will kill a man's soul," Lorelei muttered. Her ex-husband at one time blamed her for their miscarriages and even once told her that she'd robbed him of his ability to be a father. Nico said he carried a fair amount of guilt for his words, but his actions spoke a different story the moment he slept with someone else.

Lorelei gently rubbed a small circle over her belly with her thumb. It was still very possible she wouldn't carry this child to term. Her two other pregnancies she lost at nine weeks and eleven weeks respectively.

She was only a month along. Part of her wished she'd waited until she was closer to three months, but if she waited, she knew she could talk herself into not telling him at all.

And that would be a mistake.

A huge one.

Even bigger than she expected now that she'd heard this horrible story.

"You should know that Irish's mother had done the same thing that this other woman did to Irish. And then she ran off with another man and Irish hasn't spoken to her since he was a kid."

"What about his dad?" Lorelei asked.

"He drank himself to death when Irish was nineteen."

"That's horrible," she said quietly, but now she understood so much more about Irish and why he was so wounded.

"I'm just going to come out and ask," JB said. "And I'm sorry if I'm being rude and insensitive, but are you pregnant?"

"It's really none of your business," she said a little too quickly and with more snap in her tone than appropriate.

"You're right. It's not." JB inched a little closer. "But if you are, he has the right to know and he should know what you plan on doing."

"And I don't mean to be rude, but considering he's a Whiskey, it wouldn't be the first time a girl showed up on our doorstep—"

"I'm not trying to trap him," she said behind a tight jaw. "I want nothing from him. I'm just here because I thought it was best to tell him face-to-face." She sucked in a deep breath and let it out slowly. "So, obviously, I'm going to have a baby. I do plan on keeping it, but I don't expect Irish to do or be anything. I just couldn't go through life and look my kid in the eye if I didn't tell Irish. He owes me nothing."

"You made a long trip to possibly get nothing." JD

opened the door. "I'm going to call Irish. Am I telling him you're here? Or am I coming up with a different reason to get his ass back on this ranch?"

Lorelei pinched the bridge of her nose. "I don't want you to lie to your family, so you can tell him I'm here, but I would appreciate it if you didn't tell him my news."

"And if he guesses?" JD waved his hand over his head. "I'll find a way to make sure he doesn't." He shut the door.

"I'm not lying about this baby." She held her chin up and stared at JB, who had snagged his hat off the bench and adjusted it back on his head.

"No one is saying you are."

"Your brother seems to think I am."

JB squeezed her forearm. "No. He's just frustrated because even though we're a few years older than Irish, the three of us were pretty close growing up and the last year Irish has really pulled away from the family. When he retired from the Army, that was a big red flag. While we were excited to have him come home, we're concerned about what the driving force was and the fact that I've known part of it and didn't tell anyone pisses my brother off."

"It was hard not to take that personally."

JB lifted her suitcase. "Come on. I'll take you to the cabin and you can get settled in, and then I'll

come get you around seven. You can have dinner
with me and my family."

"I don't want to burden you and—"

"I insist and my wife won't take no for answer.
Trust me on this."

"I guess I have to eat sometime." She had no
energy to argue and her stomach was growling.

72

6

*T*rish rubbed his eyes, but it didn't help take the sting out. He'd been driving now for fourteen hours straight.

Why the hell was he being summoned to Whiskey Ranch?

And not just by one of his cousins.

All of them had called telling him he had to get home, but not a single one would say why. Just that it was important. That they had some news that could only be shared in person.

Well, they'd told him his father had died over the phone. Of course, he'd been in Germany when that happened.

Perhaps his mother had returned.

That was the only thing he could think of.

Shit. Renee Harper was the last person he wanted

73

to see. Ever. If she was his family's big news, he'd be surprised seeing as though they disliked her just as much. But it would make sense that they wouldn't tell him because he might not come running home.

He took the turn into the ranch with a little too much speed. The tires on his Jeep kicked up some loose gravel. The stars filled the night sky. He glanced at the digital clock on the dashboard.

Three in the morning.

He could snag a few hours of sleep before meeting his family for breakfast at Luke and Georgia Moon's place. He'd given them an ETA of zero eight hundred, only that was factoring in stopping somewhere to sleep.

He hadn't done that.

Dimming his headlights, he navigated his way to the old cabin that he and his father used to live in. JW told him when he left that would always be his home if he ever decided to return. In the last fifteen years, they'd used the cabin for visitors, special guests, and family. Otherwise, it was just sitting there, waiting for Irish to return.

Because JW knew he would.

Not because he didn't believe that the Army wasn't a good fit—JW saw that immediately after boot camp —but because JW knew this land was in Irish's blood.

But that wasn't the sole reason for his return.

And if Irish knew why he'd become so restless in the last year, he wouldn't be driving around the country aimlessly trying to figure out why his heart hurt so much.

He smiled as he rolled his Jeep to a stop under the carport next to the cabin where his cousins had left the front porch light on. He reached to the back seat and snagged his rucksack and doubled-timed it to the front door. He yawned and stretched as soon as he stepped into the foyer.

The cool air from the air conditioning system hit his skin.

He bet the fridge was stocked as well.

Tossing his bag on the sofa, he planted his hands on his hips and stared at the steps. For his entire youth, he slept in one of the two rooms at the top of the stairs. One had a queen bed and the other had a double. He suspected not much had changed since the family room was identical to when he'd left, other than a new sofa.

But the master bedroom was on the main floor with a big walk-in closet and it had a huge soaker tub, which his body would love in the morning.

Not to mention a king-size bed that even he could get lost in.

A few memories of his parents bombarded his brain. They were never pleasant.

But he wasn't a small boy anymore and neither one of them held the power to hurt him.

Not even the one that was still living.

"Master bedroom it is," he whispered as he kicked off his boots. He pushed open the door and immediately his nostrils were assaulted with the fresh sent of lilacs. Georgia Moon, or maybe all his cousins' wives, must have put something scented like a candle in the room.

It wasn't so bad.

A nightlight glowed from the bathroom. He squinted as he sat on the corner of the bed. Bending over, he reached for his socks just as the bed moved.

Smack.

Something hard hit the back of his head.

He groaned and fell forward.

"What the fuck?" Holding the back of his head, he jumped to his feet. He grabbed the dresser to steady himself.

"I've got a gun," a familiar woman's voice screeched. "And I've called the police."

He patted the wall for the light switch and flicked it. He blinked a few times, seeing stars. His vision was a tad blurry, but there was no mistaking the beautiful lady on her knees holding one of his riding trophies in her hands. "Shit, Lorelei. You drew blood." He held out his hand. "I might need stitches, but the bigger question is what the hell are you doing here? And in my bed?" He pressed his hand back on his head. There wasn't that much blood, but it still hurt like a motherfucker and he was still seeing stars.

He fumbled his way toward the bed and sat on the edge, hoping she didn't knock him over again.

"Let me take a look." Gently, she pushed his hand away.

Closing his eyes, he tried to erase the vision of her in her tiny tank top with no bra and boy shorts that didn't leave much to the imagination.

As if he needed that to remember every curve of her sexy body.

"I think you'll live." She eased from the bed. "I'll get you some ice and a towel."

"And when you come back, you've got some explaining to do." Now he knew what the reason was his family wanted him to return, but he didn't know why Lorelei had tracked him down.

A few things came to mind, but only one made his heart race and his palms sweat. He rolled his neck, trying to conjure up another reason for her to fly across the country.

But he couldn't come up with a single one.

She padded back into the room carrying a dish-towel and a bag of ice. "Here. Put this on it."

"Thanks." He leaned back on the bed. "Now, can you please explain to me why you are at Whiskey Ranch?"

She stood in front of him with her hands folded across her middle, biting down on her lower lip. "There is no way to ease into this conversation."

"Please don't tell me you're pregnant after every-thing we talked about." He tossed the bag of ice to the bed and rubbed his temples. He didn't need to be a rocket scientist to figure this one out.

"I didn't think it was possible, but I've taken a half dozen home tests and I went to my doctor before I got on a plane to come out here."

"Why didn't you tell me before I left?"

"I tried, but you didn't come see me and the base wouldn't let me on to see you."

"You went to the base?"

"The day before you left. I also tracked down Gunny, but I was too late. He gave me the address for Whiskey Ranch and I got on the next plane."

"How long have you been here?" Not that it mattered, but he was still curious. And he was trying to compartmentalize the fact that she was carrying his child. Fear prickled his gut. A million questions rattled in his mind and he didn't like where they were taking him. He had no reason to believe she was being anything but truthful.

But he didn't trust any woman who said she was having his baby.

Not anymore.

"Two days."

"So I take it my cousins know you're pregnant."

"They figured it out." She continued to stand in the middle of the room and fiddled with her hair.

It was an annoying habit.

"How did this happen? You said you had to give yourself injections to get pregnant before." He blew out a puff of air. "Did you lie to me?" Shit. He sounded like an asshole.

"No. Trust me. I was as shocked as you."

He turned, catching her gaze. He couldn't deal with this. The last time he'd been presented with the idea of being a father, he'd actually thought about it, only to be told it was too late.

For months after Jillian aborted their baby, he mourned for something he hadn't realized he ever wanted. When he'd come out on the other end, he'd come to terms with what happened and vowed he'd never let himself be put in that situation again.

"I doubt that," he said. "What do you want from me?"

"Nothing. I just felt strongly that you should know."

He swung his feet to the side of the bed. "Nothing? You've got to be kidding me." He stood. A wave of dizziness washed over him, and he fell back.

She raced to his side, pressing her warm hands on his biceps. "Are you—"

"I'm fine." He shrugged. "I can't believe you'd fly all the way from North Carolina to Idaho for nothing. So, tell me what you really want and then, after we have a paternity test, we can work it out."

"If I hadn't already hit you over the head, I'd smack you." She turned on her heel and stomped toward the door. She paused, glancing over her shoulder. "You can have this room. I'll be making arrangements to leave first thing in the morning. Like I said, I want nothing from you. If you want to be a part of your child's life, you're welcome. But other than that, I don't need one fucking thing from you." She left the room, slamming the door behind her.

Fuck. "Lorelei. Wait." He moved as fast as his pounding head would allow. "Come on. I didn't handle that well."

"No. You didn't," she called from the top of the stairs. "But I'm also happy to take a paternity test as well. I'll call my doctor and if you'd like, since you don't trust me, you can be listening to the conversation. I wouldn't want you to think I'm trapping you or taking you for a ride."

"I guess I deserved that." He rubbed the back of his neck. "I'm sorry. I haven't slept in over a day and after the way we left things, this is the last thing I expected."

"Yeah, well. I expected a lot of things to work out differently in my life, but they didn't." She placed a hand over her stomach. "After everything I've been through, I think you can understand why I want to keep this baby."

He nodded.

"I can also appreciate why you don't want to be a father. Or why this wouldn't fit into your life. I'm not here to ruin it or ask for anything. I just felt like you're the kind of man that would want to know regardless of what I wanted to do."

"I am and thank you for that," he said. "I don't think you should race off right away." Tentatively, he climbed the stairs. "You've had a few weeks to process having a child. I've had five minutes and only after you smacked me on the head."

"I'm sorry about that."

He rested his hands on her hips. "We need to talk about this. Can you stay a few days so we can work out some things?"

She nodded.

"I'm sorry I behaved so badly. I don't believe you're trying to trap me or anything."

"If I were you, I'd think the same thing." She wrapped her arms around his shoulders and leaned in, kissing his cheek. "I'm sure you're tired. Why don't you try to get some sleep? We can talk over breakfast."

"Sounds like a plan." He jogged down the steps, pausing at the bottom. "I don't how this is going to work, but I'm not going to leave you to do this by yourself." He was going to be a father. A fact he couldn't change.

$\mathcal{T}$hus far, Lorelei hadn't any morning sickness, which she didn't know if that was a good thing or a bad thing.

Her other two pregnancies, she'd felt like shit from day one.

This one, nothing, and that scared her for one simple reason—maybe it wasn't real. And now that she'd gotten used to the idea of being pregnant, she wanted this baby more than she wanted anything.

She tapped her fingernails against the countertop as she waited for the coffee maker to finish dripping the pot of decaf. Even though she could no longer have the leaded form, she would still enjoy a cup of the bitter brew every morning.

"Should you be having that?" Irish asked as he

padded into the kitchen wearing a pair of shorts and a white T-shirt.

"It's unleaded," she said. "Would you like a cup?"

"God, no." He opened the fridge. "I hope there's some regular coffee around here somewhere."

"I'll make you some as soon as this is done."

"That would be amazing."

She pulled down a new paper filter and found the regular coffee beans. "On one condition."

"What's that?"

"You cook breakfast."

He laughed. "I can manage some eggs and looks like there is some sausage. Does that sound good?" He set some fixings on the counter. "But I was told to be at my sister's place by ten."

"Well, that was before you showed up in the middle of the night."

He rubbed the back of his head.

"I'm really sorry I hit you." She cringed.

"I didn't give you much of a choice." He ran his hands up and down her arms. "I'm glad you tried to defend yourself."

His warm tender touch made her shiver.

"Are you cold?" he asked.

"No." She wanted to take a step back and put some space between them, but she found herself being drawn closer. She missed being in his arms.

For the last month all she had thought about—dreamed about—had been what it would be like to make love to him. To hold him in her arms just one last time. She knew it was crazy to even entertain the idea that she and Irish could ever be a couple. She needed to learn to be completely independent, and he had his own issues, which she hadn't really a clue as to what they were or how they affected him on an emotional level.

All she knew or understood was that he was a wounded soul who cared deeply about other people. So much so that he tended to put himself last, even if he didn't realize that's what he'd been doing all his life.

"How are you feeling? Do you have morning sickness or anything like that?" He tucked a piece of her hair behind her ear. During their one night together, he'd been very attentive. She had no idea if he was normally like that or if it had been because of all the great sex.

Standing in the middle of the kitchen in the cabin on the ranch, she decided he was just a sweet, sensitive man who could be overly affectionate.

"I feel great," she admitted. "Which is a nice change of pace considering I had the worst morning sickness when I was pregnant the other two times."

He took a step back and scratched his scruffy

growth on his face. "I hate to bring up a painful subject, but how far along are you and how far along had you been when you miscarried?"

She swallowed her breath. It was a fair question, and she shouldn't be upset that he wanted to know. She carried his child and he appeared to be sincerely concerned. "I'm only about six weeks now, so very new. I lost my other two right before the three-month mark."

"I'm sorry if I'm being insensitive, but is there something you can do to prevent it from happening again?"

She shook her head. She wished there were some magic pill, but there wasn't, and she could sit around with her feet up all day long doing nothing and eating nothing but healthy food, and she could still end up losing this baby. "The doctors have no idea why it happened."

"Have you spoken to your doctor about this pregnancy?"

If he wasn't the father and this wasn't all new to him, she'd be super annoyed. "I have and for now, he's told me to go about life as usual, with the exception of a few things."

"And what are those, exactly?" He pulled out a frying pan and placed it on the stovetop while he cracked some eggs and scrambled them.

She set a fresh mug of coffee on the counter. "No heavy lifting. Avoid excessive exercising. Don't do anything new. Avoid stress. Those kinds of things."

"Being around me I'm sure isn't helping with the stress level."

She laughed. "That's not true." She leaned against the counter. "Though, sitting around waiting to tell you that I was pregnant didn't help."

The eggs sizzled when he tossed them into the pan. He added the sausage links to the other side and poked them with the fork. "So tell me what your plan is when it comes to having this baby."

Plan? She didn't have much of one outside of keeping it, but she had to tell him something. She could tell he needed to know that she had everything under control so he could feel good about whatever decisions he was going to make about how involved, or uninvolved, he was going to be.

"Well, it's pretty simple. I still plan on finishing my college degree."

"I didn't know that you were in school."

"I'm on summer break," she said. "But I'm studying to be a preschool teacher."

"That's cool." He sipped his coffee before setting the eggs and sausage on two different plates. "How are you going to have a baby, go to school, and work?"

It was a legit question, but she resented that he sounded like her father and not the father of her baby. "I don't have every single detail worked out, but I'm not the first single mother to have to deal with all this."

"I'm sure you're not, but I'm just trying to figure out how I'm supposed to help." He set two plates on the counter. "Good daycare can be expensive, and I can't imagine you make a lot of money."

She was so hungry she decided to ignore the insulting comment for the moment. The kitchen didn't have a table, but it did have a counter with two stools. She climbed up on one and dug a fork into the fluffy eggs. They melted in her mouth. She closed her eyes and enjoyed the flavor for a moment before blinking and turning her attention back to Irish. She took a small sip of her bitter brew. "The college has a drop-in daycare that I will look into, and I have some friends who can help out when I'm working."

"What about your apartment? It's not really the best place to—"

"Are you going to just stand there and rag on my life?" Granted, these were all concerns she had herself, but she was waiting until she got past the fifteen-week mark before she went crazy with looking for a new place to live and make major lifestyle changes.

"I'm not judging you. I'm making observations while mulling over some things I can do to make your life easier."

"Like what?" She leaned back and folded her arms.

"For starters, I can help pay for daycare and a new apartment."

"I didn't come here to ask you for money. I came here to tell you that I'm having a baby. Our baby and that if you want to be a part of his or her life, that's great. If you don't, I understand that too. It's up to you. But cutting me a check every month?" She shook her head. "That's not necessary and it's certainly not being a father."

He aggressively set his mug on the counter and glared. "You don't believe that taking care of my kid and his mother financially is being a good dad?"

She picked up a sausage link and stood. This wasn't going to end well. "Honestly, yes and no."

"What the fuck does that mean?"

"If all you're doing is paying for things, it makes you an asshole. Like I said, I came here because I didn't think it was fair to have this child and not tell you. But I also don't think it's fair to ask you for anything because I'm making a choice." She picked up a thick clump of hair and ran it through her fingers. "I believe in the whole 'it's my body so it's my choice,' only that really does suck because it takes two people for this to happen."

"But it is your body and you're the one who has to go through the pregnancy and the birth, not me. So, I get that. And I respect that."

"What if I had decided to not have this baby? How would you have reacted?" Her heart dropped to the pit of her stomach at just the thought. Bile smacked the back of her throat. It wasn't something she would ever entertain, so even saying it out loud as theoretical made her want to vomit.

He dropped his fork and blinked. "On the outside I would support your decision, but inwardly, I might struggle with the concept."

Part of her wanted to tell him she knew about what his ex-girlfriend had done, but she didn't want to toss his brothers under the bus. Not yet anyway. Maybe Irish would tell her what happened on his own. Or if he didn't, that was okay too.

He leaned against the counter, sipping his coffee and staring out the window over the sink. He looked so deep in thought she couldn't bring herself to say anything, so she picked at her food and waited.

"You know, I'd probably try to talk you out of it."

"Out of what?" she asked.

"If you wanted to terminate the pregnancy. I'd ask you not to."

She smiled, resting her hand on her stomach. Those two sentences made her morning. She would hold on to them and pull them from her memory whenever she felt like crap. "Do you mind if I ask why?"

"It's a complicated answer."

"I've got all day." She pushed her plate to the side. "I think you can understand why this baby is so important to me after all I went through with my ex-husband."

"I can," Irish said. "He's a real shit."

She let out a short laugh. "But I really don't know much about why you don't want a family or children."

He glanced at his watch and let out a long breath. "My childhood was pretty shitty. If it hadn't been for my cousins and my grandparents, I'm not sure I would have even made it to the Army."

"Why do you say that?"

He ran a hand over his face. "My mom was seventeen when she got pregnant with me. My father was twenty-one. She used to always tell me the only reason she married my dad was because the Whiskey family had money and it was too late to have an abortion."

Lorelei gasped. "That's a horrible thing to say to a child."

"My mother isn't a very nice person." Irish turned and poured himself another cup of coffee. "She went on to have numerous affairs and a few abortions. She finally left my dad when I was twelve. But my dad, he loved her, and I will never understand why. She broke him and he eventually drank himself to death."

Lorelei should feel bad that she already knew some of this about Irish and his family, but she was glad he shared it with her without her having to tell him she knew. "I'm so sorry."

"I think the hardest part was watching my father beg her not to terminate one of the pregnancies. He didn't care if he wasn't the father. He told her he would raise the child as his own. He would have done anything to keep us as a family, but she never loved him. She never wanted to marry him. But her parents would have nothing to do with her once she got pregnant. They cut her off completely."

"Where is she now?"

He shrugged. "I have no idea and I've never met her side of the family."

She pressed her hands against the counter and pushed. Slipping off the stool, she padded her way around the breakfast bar. She wrapped her arms around his shoulders, massaging gently. "I can't imagine what that had to have been like for her, or for you growing up."

He set his mug to the side and rested his hands on her hips. "She only cared about the money. Last I saw her she was running off with someone who had more than what the Whiskey family could offer. Besides, by that time, JW's parents had passed and JW was being groomed to take over the ranch and he wasn't having it with my mom or my dad. The ranch controlled their finances and that pissed off my mom."

"And your father?"

"He didn't care as long as he got his booze."

"I can understand why you hightailed it out of here when you turned eighteen." She rested her head against his broad chest.

He tightened his arms around her waist, rubbing her back with his strong hands.

It had been a long time since a man held her intimately, lovingly, and she didn't want to let go. Irish made her feel safe. There was something about him that touched her soul in a way that no other man, or person for that matter, had and she wanted to pinpoint why.

It couldn't be just because she was carrying his baby because she felt it the night they had made love.

It wasn't as strong or potent as it was right this second.

He raised his hands and cupped her face. He stared into her eyes for a long moment as if he were searching for something. His thumbs fanned gently across her cheeks. "I can't say that's why I never wanted to settle down or have a family. At least not when I left home and started my journey in the Army."

"It's a pretty good reason."

He chuckled. "I suppose it shaped the way I entered the few relationships I've had with women, but the real reason I never wanted to get married or have kids was because I saw too many of my brothers go home in body bags, leaving behind wives and babies. Being in Special Forces is dangerous and I wasn't going to do that to a family."

"That's fair and no one can fault you for that. I've never understood why people make a big deal out of anyone's life choices. I have friends who never want to have kids and for a woman, that seems to be a horrible thing. Personally, I believe to each his own."

"I have to agree with you there," he said. "You're not the first woman who has come to me and told me they were pregnant."

She opened her mouth, but he hushed her with his index finger.

"About a year ago I met this girl, Jillian. She took my breath away. It was like she reached into my body and stole my heart and soul in a matter of seconds. I had never experienced anything like it in my life."

"You were in love with this woman?" A pang of jealousy tore through her bloodstream like an out-of-control train. She took a step back, needing to put some space between her and Irish.

Thankfully, he respected her wish and released his grip.

It pissed her off that she even had this emotion, especially when she already knew about what had happened, but hearing it from Irish, and seeing the pain in his eyes made it all the more real.

"I believe I was at the time, but she killed that when she had an abortion before ever telling me she was having a baby."

"That's mean. Why did she even tell you at all?"

"Because she wanted to be reimbursed."

"That's cold." Lorelei wrapped her arms protectively around her middle.

"Turns out, Jillian wasn't much different than my mother and it made me feel like I was going to be just like my dad."

Lorelei turned and brushed away a tear that had escaped her eye. "I'm neither of those women," she whispered. "Excuse me. I need to go shower and if you don't mind, I'd like to use the one in the master."

"That's fine."

"Thank you." She scurried off toward the bedroom as more tears broke free.

"Lorelei. Wait." He followed her and curled his fingers around her biceps. "I didn't tell you that to compare you to them."

She swallowed a guttural sob. Shaking her head, she shrugged from his grip and raced down the hallway. Once inside the master bedroom, she slammed the door and locked it, collapsing to the floor. She wrapped her arms around her knees and cried. She had no idea why other than her heart broke for Irish, but it also crumbled to a million pieces for herself and her own child.

Irish was an honorable man. She bet his father was too at one point, and if he stuck around to be any kind of father to their kid, it would make him feel as though he'd somehow taken the same path.

How could she do that to him?

$\mathcal{T}$rish didn't like leaving Lorelei when she'd been so upset, especially when he'd been the one to cause the tears.

Though he didn't quite understand why.

He shoved the note he'd written under the bedroom door and headed outside.

The morning sun shone bright in the blue Idaho sky. He inhaled sharply, enjoying the honeysuckle smell. As a kid, he used to love to get up early in the morning and his grandpa would pick him up and take him to the stables. He wasn't much good at being a cowboy like his cousins, but he wasn't horrible either and he loved to be around the horses.

And he loved being around his grandpa and especially enjoyed hanging out with his oldest cousin, JW. He might have been closest in age to JB, and perhaps he and JD were better friends than anyone, but JW was his idol. He often followed him around like a pathetic puppy, especially when JW was being groomed to be the next best bull rider in all the nation.

He still held the world record and that was something for a man in his forties.

In the distance, he could see a golf cart approaching with two men sitting in the front. He jogged down the porch steps and waved.

JW jerked the cart to a stop about five feet away. "Well, look at what the cat dragged in." He jumped from the vehicle with outstretched arms.

Irish pulled his cousin in for a big bro hug, letting it linger longer than what was customary, but he didn't give a shit. The Whiskey family was close, even when they weren't. "You're looking good for an old man."

"You're not getting any younger either." JW slapped his back.

"I can't believe you're here and you don't have to leave within hours of getting in." JB tossed his cowboy hat to the back of the golf cart and yanked at Irish for another hug. "We've missed you."

"Same here." Irish rustled JB's out-of-control hair. "Does your wife like this wild, crazy look of yours?"

"She's threatening to cut it all off, but secretly she loves it," JB said. "Her only concern is Jimmy wants hair just like his daddy, so now he wants to grow his, and she's all worried he'll get teased, but you know man buns; they are all the rage."

"Oh, good Lord. Please say no to the man bun," JW said with a laugh. "So, tell me. What the hell are you doing coming home in the middle of the night and scaring our guests?"

"Someone should have told me she was here." When Irish had texted his family to let them know he'd arrived, he had to tell them he made it to the cabin; therefore, he had to inform everyone that he knew Lorelei was there.

"She wasn't sure how you'd feel about her being here and if you'd make it home faster or not," JB said.

"Wonderful. So I guess you all know why she's here?" Irish ran a hand over his freshly shaven face. He still wasn't sure how he felt about this whole baby thing. On the one hand, every time he thought about it, his heart beat a little faster and a smile tugged at the corners of his mouth.

But seconds later, he was breaking out in a cold sweat thinking about all the changes he'd have to make and should he move to North Carolina and what would he do for work there or would Lorelei consider moving out here. Hell, he didn't even know where the bulk of her family lived, something he needed to ask.

There were so many unknowns.

And then there was the concern she may miscarry again.

That thought sent a brick crash-landing in the center of his gut. That wasn't something he wanted for her because it would crush her in ways he didn't think she'd ever bounce back from. He truly believed that she thought this was her last chance at having a child.

He honestly wanted that for her.

"A rabbit doesn't need to die to figure that one out," JW said. "Where is she?"

"Taking a shower. I think." Irish plopped himself down on the back of the cart. "I might have told her too much about my past and I made her cry." He pinched the bridge of his nose. "JB knows about Jillian and what happened last year, but you don't."

"Actually, I filled everyone in the other day." JB leaned against the hood of the vehicle.

"Of course you did." Irish shouldn't be surprised by that statement, considering the events of the last couple of days, but still. It wasn't JB's story to share. But what was done was done.

"That includes Lorelei," JB said.

Irish snapped his gaze up to meet his cousin. "If

she already knows the ugly truth about my past, then why is she crying?"

"I have no idea," JW said. "But knowing how you are with women, you said something really stupid."

"I told her the truth about my mom, my dad, and what Jillian did, and how it made me feel," Irish said. "I also told her I didn't tell her that to compare her to Jillian or my mom, but she didn't really let me elaborate."

JB smacked his forehead with dramatic flair. "If you told her that you felt as though you were becoming your father in that moment, you're a real fucking dumbass."

"Well, it's true. I mean, I fell for a woman who didn't even like me for anything other than my dick, kind of like my dad did, and then she goes and has an abortion without telling me? How many times did my mom do that to my dad? I mean, of course I felt like I was becoming my..." A light bulb went off in Irish's head. "I might have a slight understanding why I upset Lorelei."

"You might?" JW asked. "Because I'm happy to clear it up for you."

Irish shook his head. "No. I get that between what happened with Jillian and Lorelei being pregnant and the fact that I never wanted a family, Lorelei might think I feel as though I am my father and it's going to end up some strange self-fulling prophecy or some such bullshit." Irish waggled his finger. "But in my defense, I only told her the stories so she'd understand…understand…" Understand what? Did he even have a clue as to what his point was anymore?

"Shit, Irish," JW said. "You're telling her why you don't want a family. You can tell us it's because of your career with the Army, which we all know and believe that's one reason, but that's the reason that became convenient. The one that didn't hurt your heart and soul to the core when you had to voice it."

"Usually I think my big brother is full of shit, but he's on point with this one," JB said. "But Jillian changed you and since I'm the only one who knows the real story there, I'm the only one who can say this."

"I don't think I want to hear it," Irish said.

"Too bad." JB folded his arms. "You left the Army because of Jillian. You told me that you wanted more out of life and she showed you that, but you just didn't know how or what more looked like."

"He said that?" JW used his thumb and made a gesture toward Irish. "Because that would be a major breakthrough if he did."

"JB is leaving out the fact I was shit-faced when I said that." Irish might have been drunk, but he wasn't so wasted he didn't remember. JB was mostly right. Jillian had flipped his world. He mourned something he didn't know he wanted and now he had something he wanted, but he was afraid to wrap his brain and heart around it because he was terrified it wasn't going to last.

But he couldn't say that to Lorelei.

She had to be worried enough about losing this child; she didn't need him to be freaking out.

But he could share with his family. At least a little bit.

"You also said you wanted to give up your womanizing ways," JB added.

"All true." Irish leaned back and put his feet up on the back of the golf cart. "And I had."

"So, what was Lorelei then?" JW sat down on an old tree trunk that had been chopped down when they were kids. He picked up a blade of grass and fiddled with it.

"Someone I tried to talk myself and her out of. But she's a hard woman to say no to," Irish said.

"Are you trying to tell us she came on to you and you tried to say no?" JW asked with wide eyes.

"That's exactly what happened. But obviously that no turned into a yes. And now we're going to have a baby, which I will be present for," Irish said.

"Does she know that?" JB asked.

"This is where it gets tricky." Irish rubbed his temples. "Her ex-husband is a real shit and put her through some really rough times. She struggled to get pregnant to begin with and then when she lost the second baby, she found out he'd been cheating."

"I hate to bring this up, but you should have her do a paternity test," JW said. "They can be done at nine weeks I believe."

"No." Irish shook his head. "At least not that early in the pregnancy and maybe not until after the baby is born."

"Why not?" JW asked.

"She had two very traumatic miscarriages and I wouldn't want to do anything that would put her at risk for that happening again." Irish's heart twisted. His chest tightened. He'd already started to feel something for what probably wasn't bigger than the size of a peanut. "This is going to sound cold and rude, but I'm trying to be supportive for her, and at the same time not become too attached. Lorelei looks and acts like a tough cookie, and she is. But I've seen her talk about what happened, and I know she's worried about losing this baby and if she does, I'm not sure she'll recover from it."

"I hate to break it to you, but you're already attached." JB strolled over to the other side of the cart and squeezed his shoulder.

Irish knew that to be a fact, but he would fight it hard. He had to. "I'm going to try to see if I can talk her into staying through the first four months of her pregnancy, or I'm going back with her to North Carolina."

"I'll get you the name of Kitty's doctor," JW said. "It's everyone else's doctor as well, so she'll be in good hands."

Irish nodded. "I might need a little help convincing her to stay."

"I'll talk to Cheyenne," JB said. "She's good at stuff like that and so is Annette."

"Oh. And before I forget." JW stood. "What do you want to do at the ranch? I mean, you haven't worked on one for fifteen years. I'm not sure what we can do with your skill set."

Irish laughed. "You can put me wherever you want except in the office with JD or at the bull riding school with Luke and Georgia Moon."

"All right, then you're with me and Cheyenne at the stables," JB said.

"You know, Lorelei is studying to be a preschool teacher. If the doctor says it's okay, maybe there's something she can do at the children's center."

"I'm sure Kitty will have something for her." JW climbed in behind the steering wheel. "You start work Monday, if you're staying."

Irish hopped off the cart. "Is dinner still on at your place tonight?"

JW nodded. "Six o'clock. And don't be late. Kitty's making shepherd's pie. My favorite."

"That dish has grown on me," Irish admitted.

"As it should, considering your damn name." JB grabbed ahold of the side of the cart as JW punched the gas. "See you later, cousin."

Irish stood at the bottom of the porch steps. He sucked in a deep breath. Time to go spread some Whiskey charm and hopefully talk Lorelei into staying.

Lorelei bent over and picked up the folded piece of paper with her name on it. She smiled. Irish had excellent handwriting. Not too many people did, especially men, or lefties, which was impressive in general.

Lorelei,

I'm sorry I upset you. That wasn't my intention. I never meant to imply that I thought you were like Jillian or my mother. You are nothing like either of them. You are kind and sweet and caring, and you are going to be a fantastic mother to our child.

She gasped and clutched her chest. And even

though that wasn't exactly what had reduced her to puddles of hormones, his words touched her deeply.

I had to step outside to talk to JB and JW for a few minutes. If I'm not here when you're out of the shower, come outside or text me. I thought maybe we could go for a walk and talk some more about things.

Irish.

He was right, they did need to talk. Because she needed to get the hell out of Idaho and back to North Carolina. Or maybe she'd go back to New York.

Not that she wanted to go back to her family with her tail between her legs. Granted, her family had been supportive enough, but there was always a bit of judgment in their tone. An extra dig when they spoke. They didn't even realize they were doing it, but their compliments always turned into a sideways criticism.

Especially her father who hadn't wanted her to get married in the first place and enjoyed the occasional I told you so.

She stepped out of the bedroom and right into a solid mass of muscle.

"We really should stop meeting this way. People will start talking."

She let out a nervous laugh.

He took her chin with his thumb and forefinger.

"I'm sorry," he whispered as he brushed his lips over hers.

Without thinking, she leaned into him, wrapping her arms around his strong middle. A slight moan vibrated in her throat as he deepened the kiss.

Being in his arms, kissing him, was dangerous. She knew she would have no willpower or control when it came to Irish. For weeks she'd been dreaming about what it would be like to be with him again. To feel his lips on her skin. His hands massaging her muscles, commanding her body to give in to her desires.

She pulled away, gasping for air. "I believe I'm a little emotional from all the pregnancy hormones."

"You're allowed." He licked his lips with a broad stroke. "Did you get my note?"

She nodded. "A walk sounds nice."

"I went ahead and made some sandwiches." He stepped around her and raced into the kitchen. "There's a creek about a fifteen-minute walk from the cabin. If you grab a blanket from the front closet, we can be out of here in a flash."

"Wow. You've thought of everything." She found a black-and-red-checkered blanket and stood by the door. Excitement bubbled through her veins. She was thrilled to be spending more time with Irish, but she needed to tell him it was time for her to return to North Carolina. She needed to get back to work and start saving some money before this baby comes along.

She didn't want to leave the ranch because it was so peaceful, but every time she was alone with her thoughts, all she could think about was losing this baby and that couldn't be good.

"All right, let's go." He tossed a backpack on his shoulder and opened the door. "We can drive if you don't think it's okay for you to walk."

"Doctor said walking is fine." She glared at him. "Trust me when I say I'm not going to do anything that will jeopardize this pregnancy."

He nodded as he placed his hand on the small of her back, where it remained for the next fifteen minutes as they walked in silence across the open grassy land. She'd seen her share of beautiful scenic mountain ranges, but nothing quite as breathtaking as those perched in the distance.

Everything about Whiskey Ranch was pure perfection, right down to the winding creek that flowed through what seemed like every nook and cranny. If she didn't know better, she'd think the ranch took up half the state.

She glanced to the north and she could see the bull riding school where Luke and Georgia Moon lived. She'd had dinner there one night. It was a gorgeous spread, only she didn't care too much for all the angry bulls, which made both Luke and JW laugh since they both thought bulls were cute and cuddly.

Not.

"This ranch is amazing." She spread out the blanket under a big tree at a bend by the creek. "And your family is adorable, though Georgia Moon is a tough read."

Irish laughed. "She takes a long time to get to know and she's as tough as nails, that one."

"JB and Cheyenne have a colorful history."

Irish nodded. "They've been through a lot of hurt, but they love each other, and if two people were ever meant to be together, it's them."

"I'd say that about all your cousins and their spouses."

"True." Irish sat down and opened up his backpack, pulling out a couple of water bottles, macaroni salad, and a couple of turkey sandwiches. "I hope you're not having any weird aversions to food."

"Nope. I'm just hungry all the time." She opened the container of salad and plopped some on her plate. She dived right in with her fork. "This is delicious."

"Kitty made it."

"She's a great cook." Lorelei continued to stuff

her face, avoiding the hard conversation she needed to have with Irish. She had no idea how he was going to take it, but he had to know it was coming. She set her plate down, keeping her sandwich in her hand, and stretched out her legs. "I was looking at flights this morning."

"I was afraid of that." Irish took a big swig of his water. "I don't think you should go until at least after we get through the first few months where the doctor believes you'll carry to term."

She choked on a piece of turkey.

Irish patted her back. "Are you okay?"

"Just slightly shocked at your terminology."

"I did some reading on the internet this morning," he said with a proud smile. "I also have the name of Kitty's and everyone else's doctor for you, and I'm sure it won't be a problem for you to get in. This family has brought him enough business."

She set her food back down and wiped her hands. "You're being a bit overbearing. My ex was controlling and I hated that."

He held up his hands. "I'm not trying to control anything. I'm only trying to look out for you and our baby's best interest while also trying to be a part of it all."

"So, you really want to be in this kid's life?" she asked. So far, he'd never really come out and said it, and if they were going to seriously continue this discussion, it needed clarification.

"I do. I have no idea how it's going to work, but for now, I'd really like it if you'd consider staying at the ranch for a few months. I know your job could be an issue, but I've got money and I plan on helping out financially, whether you like that or not. I mean it's what dads do."

She blinked a few times. "And if I said no to staying?"

"I'd go back to North Carolina with you."

"What if I stay until I get past the first three months, but go back after that? Then what?"

He ran a hand over his jaw. "I don't know. I have a job here at the ranch for the rest of my life if I want it. I also have two other job offers working for private bodyguard type firms that I could do and work at the ranch, which would be a great gig for me and a lot of money. I have no job offers in North Carolina, but I haven't looked, so that's something for me to consider."

"I can't ask you to change your plans or uproot you—"

He pressed his finger over her lips. "Both our lives just got a bit uprooted by what's growing in that belly of yours. I'd say our lives are changing no matter what we do. So, we need to think about what's best for all of us, not just one of us."

"But we're not even a couple."

"No. We're not. But like I said. Different time. Different place." He raised his palms to the sky. "Maybe this is our time and place. I have no idea. But we're in this together."

She blew out a puff of air and stared at the big blue sky. A few birds flew overhead. The idea of being on her feet all day at a hostess job during the first three months didn't thrill her, but sitting around a ranch doing nothing wasn't all that exhilarating either.

"I can tell you're thinking about everything, so let me toss one more thing at you." Irish moved closer, putting his arm around her waist. "I'm sure you received the grand tour of the ranch when you got here."

"I did."

"So, you saw the children's center."

"Oh my, yes. Kitty has done an amazing job with that place. It's like you have your own little city right here on the ranch."

"Exactly," Irish said. "And as long as the doctor okays it, JW said Kitty might have a job for you at the preschool or daycare center."

"You really do think of everything, don't you?"

He laughed. "I'm not trying to be too pushy, but I think this would be a good environment for you." He lay down on the blanket, put his head in her lap, and stared up at her with warm, loving eyes. "I know what this baby means to you and I want to do everything in my power to make sure these first few worrisome months aren't so troublesome for you."

She leaned over and kissed his forehead. "That's the sweetest thing anyone has ever said or done for me." She threaded her fingers through his hair, which had grown about a half inch since he'd left the Army, and she liked it this length. "But I can't stay here forever. I have school and—"

"There are colleges in Idaho. Ask Kitty. She transferred and did her master's degree here."

"Now you're being controlling and pushy."

He smiled. "Does that mean you're going to stay for the next two months?"

"More like six weeks, but yes. I'll stay."

Lifting his head, he cupped the back of her neck, drawing her lips to his in a sweet, tender kiss. Quickly, it turned wild and passionate and their tongues danced a familiar waltz and his hand made its way down toward the swell of her breast and her tightening nipple.

She grabbed his wrist. "The last time we did this, I got knocked up."

"The good news is right now that can't happen, so we have nothing…" He frowned. "We shouldn't be having sex. Not during the first three months."

"There is nothing that says we can't."

"I want to hear that from a doctor before we do that."

She jerked her head back. "Are you seriously turning down sex in broad daylight by a creek when I'm hoping you haven't had it since the last time I saw you?"

"I haven't been with anyone since you, and that better be the case—"

"You have nothing to worry about. Now how about I go changing your mind." She took his hand and pressed it against her chest.

He yanked it away. "Call the doctor. Make an appointment and we can ask about sexual activities. And then you can put my hands wherever your heart wants."

She sighed. She found him way too genuine to keep pushing. And maybe he had a point. She'd only seen her doctor once and it might be a good idea to get a second opinion. "I'm going to hold you to that."

9

*T*rish curled his fingers around the door handle and stepped into the cabin. He wanted to yell *honey, I'm home,* but refrained. It didn't feel right.

Nothing felt right.

Except for when he had Lorelei in his arms, but every time he did that, he was reminded she could lose this baby, or that he didn't deserve her. She was way out of his league and he didn't know how he was going to be the kind of man that she would want to be with for the rest of her life.

And they barely knew each other.

"Hey, you," she said with a big smile as she looked up from her book. "How was your day?"

"Grueling," he admitted. "I swear JW is playing

payback for me leaving for fifteen years with what he has me doing."

"I doubt that."

Irish kicked off his boots and set them back out on the porch. He'd clean them off later. "I took out some steak this morning that I'll grill for dinner."

"I saw that, so I brought back some fresh beans when I went to town with Annette today."

He cocked his head. "You went where?"

"Relax. We went to a coffee shop to hang out for a little bit and then the fresh market. I didn't do anything strenuous."

"I wish you would have told me." He rubbed the back of his neck. Tomorrow's doctor's appointment couldn't come soon enough. He desperately needed to know what she could do and what she couldn't, and a quick phone call from the nurse telling him it was okay for her to be around babies at the daycare or to do daily activities didn't cut it.

He needed more information.

And he needed her to have a full exam.

If only for his peace of mind. Everyone else on this ranch might have been through this, but he hadn't so they needed to cut him some slack.

"I don't need to check in with you on every little thing I do."

He pinched the bridge of his nose. "No. You don't

and I smell like horse shit so I'm going to go take a shower."

"That sounds like a good idea because the stink is making me nauseous."

He chuckled and was grateful for the light humor. He made his way into the master bathroom. For the most part, she stayed in that bedroom alone, though he sometimes allowed himself to fall asleep with her, though not the last night or two, simply because he wasn't strong enough anymore to keep his hands to himself.

Something was going to happen if he kept waking up with her in his arms and he'd never forgive himself if she lost this baby because of his selfishness.

He stripped off his muddy clothes and put them in the hamper, which he'd bring to the laundry room before starting dinner. The corners of his mouth tugged into a smile. He had to admit, in a very short time period, he'd come to enjoy this lifestyle. He didn't mind that right now he was carrying most of the workload between working as ranch hand and coming home and cooking and cleaning.

He enjoyed taking care of Lorelei.

He just wished he was good enough for her and no amount of money would make him the kind of man she deserved.

Stepping in the shower, he let the hot water melt away the ache in his muscles.

The sound of the door opening and closing made him jump. He blinked, wiping his eyes. "Lorelei. What the hell are you doing?"

She slipped out of her sundress and panties and stepped into the shower. Her hair cascaded over her round plump breasts, which he'd noticed had gotten bigger.

He took a step back.

"I thought you might need a hand getting all that filth off your body."

He swallowed. Hard. "This isn't a good idea." He rubbed his forefinger and thumb together, trying not to stare at her puckered nipples, but it proved impossible.

"What are you so afraid of?"

"I can't believe you just asked me that." He reached around her and shoved open the door. Grabbing a towel, he wrapped it around her body and gently lifted her from the shower, landing her feet on the bath mat. "I won't take the risk until we know for certain it's safe and even then, I think it's best if we wait until after you get past the three-month mark."

"Or maybe you just don't want me and this is all a fucking excuse." She turned and stormed out of the bathroom, slamming the door so hard it rattled the mirror.

"Shit, that didn't go too well," he muttered as he quickly finished washing. It was the fastest shower he'd ever taken and he'd barely taken the time to dry off. By the time he'd made it back out into the family room, she was nowhere to be found.

But she'd left him a note on the kitchen counter.

Irish,

I made myself a salad and went upstairs. I took the smaller room but you can have the master tonight if you want. It's been a long day and I'm tired. I'll see you at three fifteen when you pick me up for the doctor's—that is if you still want to go. It's okay if you don't. Just text me if you've changed your mind. I'll just need to borrow your car.

Lorelei.

"Oh, for fuck's sake." He stomped up the stairs. "Open the door, Lorelei."

"I'm tired," she said. "I left you a note."

"I read your fucking note and I don't do passive aggressive bullshit. Now open the damn door." He waited about three minutes before she complied, but barely.

She stuck her head out and it was obvious she'd been crying.

Fuck. He'd gone and done it again.

"Why the hell would you think I've changed my mind?"

"Because you've done an about-face with a lot of things lately."

He sucked in a deep breath and let it out slowly. "Like what?" It was rare he ever lost his temper with anyone, much less a woman, but he had no idea what he'd done that was so horrible this time.

"The first few nights here, you'd fall asleep with me, but the last few nights, you can't wait to get out of bed and go upstairs."

He planted his hands on his hips. "Please tell me how that's me doing any kind of flip. I'm just trying to be respectful."

"By rejecting me?"

"That's what you think I'm doing?" Tentatively, he pushed open the door and drew her close, gently kissing her sweet lips. "I'm sorry if that's how all this comes across."

"It's not just that. I felt like we had a connection but now all you do is avoid me. I can't do this. Maybe I should go back to North Carolina."

"Is that what you want?" He dropped his hands to his sides and took a step back. "Because all I want is for you and our baby to be safe, healthy, and happy." His heart grew heavy. If she really wanted to go, he'd have to let her. He couldn't keep her at the ranch if she was that miserable. It wouldn't be good for her or the baby. "I'm trying to do what's best for all of us, but I can't force you to stay no matter how much I want you to."

"It doesn't feel like you want me at all," she said. "And as far as the baby goes, my life is in North Carolina. It took me a long time to establish myself there, but I have friends who can help and support me. I have a job, a good one, and Candice is willing to let me have whatever hours I need to fit my schedule. I have—"

He raised his hand. "I get it. You don't like it here and want to go back. Let's talk to the doctor tomorrow and I'll see about getting a job in North Carolina."

She grabbed his arm. "You don't have to uproot your life here. I can tell how much you love it."

He cocked his head. "You accused me of rejecting you and avoiding you, which neither are true. And yet here you are, telling me you want to leave and for me not to come with you. That sounds like rejection to me." He spun on his heel and was down the stairs and had his hand on the front door.

"Irish, that's not fair."

"Neither was your note," he said under his breath. "I'm going out for a bit. Don't wait up." He slammed the door shut and stood on the porch, wondering where the fuck to go because heading to a bar wasn't appealing and being around any of his cousins at the moment didn't excite him either.

So, he made himself comfortable on the front porch swing and stared at the stars, hoping they might speak to him and give him a suggestion on what to say to Lorelei.

Lorelei sat in the infant room at the daycare center, rocking one of the babies as she fed the little boy a bottle. The boy's name was Hercules and he was the son of one of the horse trainers on the ranch. He was only eight weeks old and this was his second time at the center.

The children's center was more of a massive campus that housed not only a daycare center, but an elementary school for all the families that lived and worked at the ranch. Even people who came to train could bring their kids and enroll them into the school.

It also had special tutoring for middle school and high schoolers, along with a charter school for those age groups. Kitty had also made available home-school and GED programs for students needing alternative education.

Not to mention all the college prep courses.

There wasn't any need for a child to step off Whiskey Ranch to get an excellent education. As a matter of fact, Kitty provided one of the most comprehensive programs in the state, and she'd won an award for it.

"Isn't he adorable," Kitty said as she stepped into the room with a bright smile. Her wavy red hair bounced over her shoulders. She was always a walking ball of fiery happiness.

Lorelei had never met anyone so positive and full of sunshine before. Kitty was the kind of person that made everyone feel good, even when their mood had been shit.

"What baby isn't?" Lorelei took the bottle and set it on the table while she put the half-asleep child over her shoulder and patted his back gently. "I could sit in here all day."

"I know the feeling." Kitty took the boy and set him in one of the cribs. "It's rare that all infants are asleep at the same time."

"I'm sure one of them will be waking up soon."

"Well, I learned the hard way that you should never wake a sleeping baby when I had my first kid." Kitty pulled up a chair. "How are you feeling? Any morning sickness or anything yet?"

Lorelei had been on the ranch now for about two

weeks and she was close to being two months pregnant. The closer she got to nine and eleven weeks, the harder it became to sleep or concentrate on anything. She was just waiting for history to repeat itself and part of why she threw herself at Irish was because she wanted to get lost in something good. Something that made her feel alive. Desired. Something that made her feel like she was a whole woman. "I feel fine."

Kitty tilted her head. "I sense a tone in the word *fine*. What's going on?"

Lorelei shouldn't say anything but she needed to talk to someone. "Irish is making me nuts by doing literally everything for me and four o'clock can't come soon enough so that the doctor will tell him I'm not going to break if I make my own breakfast. This morning, when I woke up, there were pancakes in the fridge. All I had to do was heat them up."

"That's cute."

"The first three mornings I thought so too. But he's not happy that I'm here a few hours every day. And I can't believe I'm going to tell you this." She leaned forward, making sure no one else was in earshot. "You can't tell anyone. Especially your husband."

"I don't tell him girl things. It makes him break out in hives."

Lorelei laughed. "Irish won't have sex with me."

"Excuse me?" Kitty stared at her with wide eyes. "You've got to be kidding me."

"I wish. At first, I thought it was because he was afraid I'd miscarry, which I guess is valid considering how little he knows about women, babies, and well, anything related to all of that. But now I think he's using it to avoid me because the closer we've gotten to this appointment, the weirder his behavior. Like he used to come into the master and watch TV with me and *accidentally* fall asleep. Now he leaves as soon as the show is over and sleeps upstairs. It's like he's afraid the doctor's going to say go ahead, bone her, and he's going to be like, but I don't want to because I don't even like her."

"Well, I don't know Irish very well. But JW and his siblings all say they've never seen him so smitten before."

"You could have fooled me." Lorelei let out a long breath and dropped her head back. "I got naked yesterday and joined him in the shower. He looked mortified and wrapped me in a towel and told me no. Not until the doctor says it's okay. I'd never been so humiliated in all my life. I told him I should go back to North Carolina. He didn't say I shouldn't."

"I feel like you're leaving out some of the conversation because I don't believe for one second Irish wants you to leave this ranch. As a matter of fact, I know for certain he wants you to stay well beyond the three-month mark of your pregnancy."

"We'll, he has a funny way of showing it."

"Did it ever occur to you that he's scared?"

"Of what?"

"Losing you and the baby."

Lorelei stopped rocking and stared at Kitty. "Then why would he say he'd go look for a job in North Carolina?"

"Because he'll do anything to be near you."

"No. He wants to be near his baby. I have accepted the fact he wants to be in this kid's life, which is a good thing and I'm all for it. But he doesn't want me," Lorelei said. "If I had gone back to North Carolina and been on my own turf, maybe I would have never fallen so hard for him."

"Fallen? As in love?"

"I don't know," Lorelei said. "We spent one amazing night together where we thought we'd never see each other again. It allowed us to really open up to one another. I think we told each other things we wouldn't have dreamed of telling someone else."

"What did Irish say to you that was so revealing?" Kitty scooted her chair closer. "I'm sorry. I shouldn't have asked that, but he's kind of an enigma. Even JW says that, though JB and JD know him differently, I guess."

"It was how he wanted to be a different kind of man than he'd always been." Lorelei had been thinking a lot about what she'd learned about Irish and one thing that struck her was something that Irish hadn't even put together yet himself. But she knew it to be true. "He saw himself as this love 'em and leave 'em kind of person. He even said he wasn't a nice man. But when he told me about this Jillian person, he worried he was becoming like his father. At first, I worried that I was going to make him feel that way. But then I realized I was more worried I was making him feel trapped."

"Like his mother," Kitty interjected.

"And she was a love 'em and leave 'em type of woman," Lorelei said. "I think Irish has gone through life with an empty heart, even though he loves deeply, like I believe his father had, and you all do, but he somehow managed to believe he doesn't deserve it."

Kitty took her hand. "That's very different from him not wanting to be with you."

"But he has to see he's worthy of love or he won't ever be able to love back." Lorelei fought the tears that threatened to break free. "And I can't sit around here and feel horrible about myself anymore."

Kitty wrapped her arms around Lorelei. "Running away isn't the answer. You have to tell him how you feel and before any decisions are made."

Lorelei knew Kitty was right. She would have to swallow her pride and make herself even more vulnerable. If Irish rejected her, she'd have to deal with it.

A knock came at the door and one of the other daycare providers stuck her head in. "Irish is here," she said.

Kitty nodded. "I've got the infant room covered. You go ahead."

"Wish me luck," Lorelei whispered as she stood, smoothing down her slacks. Between the doctor's appointment and speaking with Irish about her feelings, it was going to be one hell of a roller-coaster ride of an afternoon.

10

*T*rish paced in the waiting room while the doctor did Lorelei's exam. He had no idea what to expect, even though he'd been studying that damn what to expect book.

It told him nothing.

It was like reading something in a foreign language.

Not only did he not understand women, he didn't understand their bodies, which was a big blow to his male ego.

"Mr. Whiskey?" a woman called from behind the desk. "The doctor said you can join Miss Sheldon now."

"I don't know where I'm going." He rubbed his hands nervously on his thighs.

"You can follow me."

"Thanks." He strolled through a maze of hallways, dodging a few pregnant women, all with their hands on their bellies. He tried not to stare, but he was in awe of the beauty that was motherhood. In the past, he'd never given it much thought. Not even with his cousins, except for when those little buggers were born. He loved all his little second cousins and he enjoyed playing with them.

But he could give them back to their parents. He wasn't responsible for their well-being. However, he did enjoy getting them all riled up and filled with sugar and then watching their parents try to deal with the aftermath.

Payback might be a problem.

The young lady knocked at the door. "I have Mr. Whiskey with me."

"Great. Send him in," Dr. Amerces said.

"Is everything okay?" Irish stood at the side of the exam table and took Lorelei's hand, running his thumb in a tender circle over her skin. "Are there any problems or concerns?"

"None that I can see, but I know you're both concerned about Lorelei's history," Dr. Amerces said. "I concur with her previous physician that she does not have a weak or incompetent cervix."

"I'm sorry, Doc. You're going to have to treat me like I'm a two-year-old." Irish swallowed. "I know what a cervix is, but not exactly sure what you mean by the rest of it."

"Basically, if Lorelei had a compromised cervix, it could cause her to miscarry, though that does generally happen more often in the second trimester."

With his free hand, he pinched the bridge of his nose. He was going to be a nervous wreck for the next seven months. "Is that something we should worry about?"

"I don't think so." The doctor moved some machine closer to the side of the table.

"But you don't know that for sure, do you?"

Lorelei, who hadn't uttered a single word since he stepped into the room, dropped her head back and groaned. "Do you see what I'm working with here, Doctor?"

"All the Whiskey men are a little overbearing and worrywarts when it comes to their wives having babies. It comes with the territory." The doctor lifted Lorelei's shirt.

"I think Irish has put new meaning into the word *worry*," Lorelei muttered.

The doctor let out a soft chuckle.

Irish didn't see what was so funny.

"Lorelei has already heard the heartbeat," the doctor said. "I'm guessing that you'd like to take a listen, Dad?"

Irish coughed on his breath. "You already heard it?" He stared into Lorelei's soft eyes.

Tears pooled in her gentle orbs. She nodded. "I wanted to make sure before I brought you back."

He inhaled sharply and squeezed her hand.

She gripped harder.

The doctor put some kind of jelly on her stomach before rolling a device on her skin.

The *thump*, *thump* of a tiny little heart filled the room.

Goosebumps dotted Irish's body. "Is that our baby?"

She nodded. "He or she is strong," she whispered.

"Everything sounds and looks good. I'll want to see her back in four weeks, unless something happens." The doctor removed the listening device. "In the meantime, I don't want her lifting anything heavy. Certainly, I'd prefer her not to be riding horses, or doing any activities she hasn't done in the past."

"I do everything around the house, so she doesn't have to lift a finger."

The doctor smiled. "There's no reason she can't do light housework. And she tells me she's working at the preschool/nursery on the ranch, which I think is great. I don't want her to be completely idle."

Lorelei waved her hand. "I can't stand it when

people talk about me as if I'm not in the room." She took the tissue that the doctor offered and wiped off her stomach, pulling down her shirt, then swung her legs to the side of the exam table.

"Sorry," the doctor said. "The point is we have no idea what caused the miscarriages. It could have been nature's way of saying there was something wrong with the fetus."

"But twice?" Irish asked.

"It happens," the doctor said. "And that doesn't mean it will happen this time. However, you both should go about your lives without stressing too much about it."

"Easier said than done, Doc." Irish looped his arm around her waist, resting his hand on the small of her back. He wanted to ask about sex, but he didn't want to seem overly eager either. And he wasn't sure he could actually go through it; he was still so worried he would cause a problem and he'd never forgive himself. "What else can I do to help Lorelei?"

"You're doing it." The doc squeezed his shoulder. "Just be there for her, support her, but don't suffocate her."

"That's not likely to happen," Lorelei muttered.

He snapped his gaze to hers, wondering what the hell that was supposed to mean, but he wasn't about to ask. Not in front of the good doctor. "What else can't she do?"

"Nothing, really. She should live her life normally." The doc leaned in. "I think I know where this is going." He smiled. "If you're worried about sex, it's perfectly fine and safe. The only thing I'd say is I'd avoid anything too rough."

She arched a brow and tilted her head.

He tried to keep from smiling, but he felt the corners of his lips moving in an upward direction. "Is there anything else I should know?"

"I think that's it," the doctor said. "Stop by the appointment desk on your way out. I want to see you in no less than four weeks."

"Thanks, Doctor Amerces." Lorelei hopped from the exam table. "I appreciate you taking me on as a patient."

"It's my pleasure," the doctor said. "See you soon."

Irish opened the door and followed her through the maze of hallways, astonished that she even knew how to find her way back to the front of the building. She made an appointment for a little more than three weeks out, which pleased Irish.

He opened the door, and the warm air smacked his face. A breeze kicked up, sending the fresh smell of lilies to his nose. "So, this means you're staying."

"At least through the first three months, it does."

He opened the passenger door of his Jeep. "That makes me happy."

"Why?"

"Because I want to take care of you and our baby."

"That's the only reason?" she asked.

"Isn't that the best reason?"

"It's one reason, but I wouldn't say it's the best, or what I necessarily want to hear."

"I don't know what you want me to say and I'm tired of trying to figure it out," he said, helping her into the seat and pulling the buckle across her lap. "I wish you would just tell me what I'm doing wrong."

She snagged it from his grasp. "I'm a grown-ass woman. I can buckle myself."

He stepped back and raised his hands. "I guess I'm not coming out of the doghouse anytime soon."

"Ya think?"

Perhaps it was time to call in reinforcements. Maybe Georgia Moon might be able to shed some light on whatever the fuck it was that he was doing wrong.

He slipped behind the steering wheel and pressed the start button. Or maybe, the surprise he had back at the house might be just what the doctor ordered. Of course, he had to sneakily text Cheyenne and JB to go ahead with the plan since all was well at the doctor's office.

Irish punched the gas and pulled out of the parking lot and onto Main Street. "I'm really trying here and I wish you could see that."

"I never said you weren't meeting my needs or taking care of me and the baby."

"That's not what I meant." He blew out a puff of air. He probably shouldn't bring this up, but he wanted so desperately to clear the air. "But ever since yesterday, you've been so upset with me and I honestly don't think I deserve it."

"I shouldn't have to explain this to you." She crossed her legs and folded her arms.

Not a good sign.

However, he wasn't going to say another damn word. His mouth seemed to get him into trouble, so maybe his grand gesture might speak better for him.

It was at least worth a try.

Lorelei gave herself a mental tongue-lashing. Irish was right. He didn't deserve her continued anger. And it wasn't that she was all that mad. No. She was afraid he would reject her again or worse.

That even if he did want her, his attraction

wouldn't last very long. Soon, her belly would grow and he might not find her sexy enough to stick around. Of course, if all they had was raw sex appeal, then they really had nothing to build any kind of relationship on.

Besides, Irish wasn't the kind of man that stayed put very long, something she was learning the hard way. It wasn't something anyone said, because not a single one of his family spoke ill of him, though she did get the impression they all believed he'd ran from home the first chance he got.

No one blamed him, not even JW, though they all wished he'd come home a lot sooner.

However, the more she and Irish lived under the same roof, the more awkward things became, and she knew she wasn't the only one feeling it because he acted oddly at the strangest of times. It was the little things like when he pulled away while they were in the kitchen and teasing each other while doing the dishes.

She glanced out the window as they pulled into the ranch's main entrance. "Wow. Look at that sky."

"I know. I've been all over the world, but nothing beats an Idaho sunset."

"God, that just makes me crave a loaded potato."

He laughed. "That might be on the dinner menu."

"I'm going to be one fat pregnant woman with you as my cook."

He patted his ripped abs. "I'm not doing my stomach any favors either." He turned down the long narrow road that led to the far corner of the ranch where their cabin was located. It was in a moment like this where she felt like they could ease back into their playful ways. Only if she allowed herself to let her guard down, he'd only hurt her feelings in the end.

She couldn't keep on the roller-coaster ride. She needed to protect her feelings if she were to get through the first few months of this pregnancy. Once she felt safe that she was going to carry this baby, then she'd be tougher and have the conversation that was going to tear her heart to shreds.

Irish rolled the Jeep to a stop under the carport and jumped out, racing across the hood of the vehicle.

She bit back her annoyance, trying to remind herself that two weeks ago his gentlemanly ways made her smile. And what honestly had changed? Her or him?

"Thank you." She took his hand and did her best to make an attitude adjustment. Oh, how she wished she could have a glass of wine. That used to always help calm her nerves. She glanced up, seeing

Cheyenne step from the porch. That's when Lorelei noticed a horse grazing in the front yard. "What are you doing here?"

"How did things go at the doctor's?" Cheyenne asked.

"Great. We got to hear the heartbeat." Irish pressed his hand on the center of her back. "I've never heard anything so amazing."

"It is pretty cool." Cheyenne undid the reins that had been looped around the tree and quickly mounted her horse. "I better get going. I have to pick up Jimmy from bull riding school."

"Doesn't it scare you that he might get hurt?" Lorelei asked.

Cheyenne let out a dry laugh. "Of course it does, but I'd be a hypocrite considering I'd broken my arm and wrist by the time I was his age bronc riding not to mention all the injuries my husband had." She waved her hand. "Though some of those were at the hands of his siblings or because JB just doesn't have the best judgment at times."

"I'll go more with the latter," Irish said with a hearty laugh. "See you later."

Cheyenne kicked the sides of her horse and took off in a trot toward the house she and her family lived in on the other side, without ever telling Lorelei why she'd stopped by.

Something Lorelei really wanted an answer to. "Why was she here? And in your cabin?"

"Let's go in and find out." He nudged her up the steps.

"What are you up to, Irish Whiskey?"

"Why do I have to be *up to* anything?"

She paused at the front door and tilted her head. "I might not know you all that well, but I can tell by that stinking prideful grin on your face that you've done something and that sort of frightens me."

"Why on earth would that scare you?" He pulled open the door and waited for her to enter.

She stood her ground, staring at him.

"Aren't you going to go inside?" he asked with a twinkle in his dark orbs. He was like a little boy who'd just walked into a video game store and was told that everything was free and he could take everything he wanted.

"Do I have to?"

"No, but you might want to. I have it on good authority that there are creamy potatoes au gratin in the oven."

She stuck her head in the door and took a big sniff. Immediately her senses were assaulted with the scents of fresh asparagus, cheesy potatoes, and grilled meat.

Her favorites.

"Feeding me my favorites does not get you off the hook." She tossed her purse on the table by the door and took three steps when she paused midstep and gasped. She clutched her chest and glanced around the room, which was filled with balloons and flowers.

And not just any flower.

Her favorite.

Gardenias.

In the corner, on the rocker, was a huge stuffed gorilla.

"How did you know I liked gorillas?" she whispered.

"I called your friend Candice."

She glanced up at Irish. "That's got to be one of the sweetest things anyone has ever done." She wiped the tear that escaped her eye and rolled down her cheek. "Damn hormones have me nuts."

"Can I ask you a question without you getting upset with me?"

"I can't guarantee I won't be mad."

"Fair enough," Irish said. "Were you this emotional with the other two pregnancies?"

"No. Actually, I don't believe I was."

"Maybe that's a good sign." He wrapped his arms around her waist. "Though it kind of sucks for both of us because I feel so bad that you're all over the map with your feelings, and well, I'm afraid to open my mouth in fear I'm going to piss you off."

"Have I really been that bad?" She turned and rested her hands on his shoulders, leaning into his strong frame.

"No. I'm sure I deserved some of it." He kissed her nose. "I have no idea what I'm doing. Not when it comes to being with someone who is pregnant. Hell, I have no clue how to be in any kind of relationship."

She blinked.

A few times.

There is no way he meant that they were in an actual serious committed anything. The only thing she ever asked of him was if he was going to be in their kid's life that he didn't become one of those fathers that breezed in and out whenever the wind blew. That if he was going to make an effort, he did so wholeheartedly. She understood that if he chose to stay in Idaho, she in North Carolina, that there would be some major hurdles to overcome when it came to visitation, but technology would allow for videoconferencing calls and other forms of communication.

Not to mention he wasn't poor and he could afford to travel back and forth and was willing to do so, or so he said.

"However, you do tend to be overbearing and controlling at times." She might as well be honest, considering he was giving her the option.

"I can work on that. But you do understand it's just because I'm worried about you and the baby." He took her by the hand and led her toward the kitchen.

More tears filled her eyes as she stared at the table which had already been set with a dozen red and white roses in a vase in the middle.

"You really can be a sweet man when you want to be."

"I always want to show that side when I'm with you." He pulled out a chair. "Why don't we have a nice dinner and—"

"It can be reheated, right?"

"I'm sure it can, but Cheyenne and JB went to a lot of trouble…" He let his words trail off as he ran a hand through his hair. "You don't want to eat right now, do you?"

She shook her head. "You heard what the doctor said about sex."

Irish nodded. His face turned serious.

"I'd rather go to the bedroom."

Irish's eyes widened. "Let me turn off the oven and remove the steaks so they don't turn to rubber."

"I'll go get naked."

Irish groaned. "That's not making me care about the steaks."

"I'm only concerned about the potatoes and sex." She toyed with the hem of her shirt, lifting it higher, exposing her bra.

"You're not making me want to salvage any of our dinner that I asked Cheyenne and JB to help with."

"Do whatever you want." She smiled, tossing her shirt across the room. Reaching behind her back, she unhooked her bra and let it drop to her feet.

"Good Lord, woman. You are either trying to kill me or starve me."

She wasn't about to wait and find out what he was going to do with the food, because if she did, it might destroy her emotions. So, she turned on her heel and hightailed it to the master bedroom, praying he was only a couple steps behind.

Although, if he took a few moments to save their dinner, she wouldn't be upset.

11

For the next few weeks, Irish couldn't believe how happy he'd been. If he'd known being with a woman could be so rewarding, he would have given being in love a second try a long time ago. Except, there was only one Lorelei and he couldn't imagine he could ever love anyone else.

Of course, he'd yet to tell Lorelei how much he really cared for her and he ran the risk she didn't feel the same way. For all he knew, this was just pretend for while she hung out at the ranch. She still occasionally talked about when she returned to North Carolina, especially when referencing her college education, something he fully supported. Only, he hoped she'd consider doing it in Idaho.

He'd even gone as far as to ask Kitty if she'd be

willing to discuss what universities might have programs that would interest Lorelei, but he hadn't heard if that conversation had taken place and what, if anything, had come from it.

But if she had her heart set on returning to the Carolinas and living there, he had already started looking for opportunities for employment. He didn't want to leave the ranch, or his family, but he would for her.

And his baby.

They were his family now.

He needed to make sure Lorelei and his baby were his focus. Everything else came in second and no one should fault him for that. If they did, too freaking bad.

He stretched, rolling to his side, pulling Lorelei into his arms. "Good morning, sunshine."

"There is no sun peeking through that window."

He chuckled. "Maybe not, but the sky is turning a lighter shade and you're awake, so I know it's morning."

"Only because I got up to pee twenty minutes ago."

"You are the best alarm I've ever had."

"You are so weird."

"I take that as the highest form of a compliment anyone could ever give me." In the last few weeks, he'd had more sex than he'd had in the last six months. Not that he was counting and not that it mattered how many times. It could have been once and that's all he needed.

Or desired.

But he had a hard time turning her down.

However, he didn't struggle with making it soft and tender, even when she tried to entice him to be wild and rough.

He'd save that for after the baby was born. Only he wasn't sure she was going to stick around, or that he'd be welcome in her life in North Carolina.

A topic they still danced around and every time he brought it up, either something or someone got in the way or she brushed it under the rug, wanting to wait until she was closer to thirteen or fourteen weeks before having that conversation.

Well, she was twelve weeks as of yesterday, according to the doctor's chart. Technically, she'd made it into the second trimester. Something she'd never done before.

He smoothed her hair away from her face, letting his hand roll down the smooth silky skin on her arm. He lifted his head off the pillow and glanced at his phone displayed on the nightstand. "You let me sleep too late."

"You needed it." She snuggled in closer, kissing the small space under his ear. "You've been working long days and then coming back here and taking care of everything." She tilted her head. "But now that I'm three months, I can start doing more, like cooking you dinner and catching up with the laundry."

"You have a doctor's appointment in three days. Why don't we keep things as they are until then?" He brushed his lips over hers, wishing he could stay in bed, but he needed to get to the main barn by six thirty. He didn't mind doing grunt work. He knew JW would make him work his way around the ranch, doing different things until he found where he fit in best. Although, he knew it would be working in the horse school, but not the one where he'd have to train cowboys and cowgirls.

No, he much preferred working with novices. Young kids and teenagers who had a fascination for horses, but didn't have the inclination, or the talent, for the circuit.

He also loved giving guided tours. That had always been his favorite when he'd been a kid growing up on the ranch.

"I suppose I can handle being pampered a little while longer." She slipped from the bed, pulling her robe over her naked body. It had already started to change, which he had to assume was a good thing. "I'll go put on some coffee while you shower."

"Thanks." He pushed himself to a sitting position and gasped when he noticed a red stain on the sheets. "Lorelei, are you bleeding?"

She glanced over her shoulder. Her sweet smile turned to a frown. Her skin paled. She grabbed her stomach as she fell to the bed.

He immediately wrapped her in his arms. "It's not a lot of blood."

"But still. That's how it starts."

"Get dressed. I'll call the doctor and tell him we're heading to the hospital."

She swiped at her cheeks. "He's just going to tell us to wait it out at home. That's what they've always had me do in the past. Besides, there isn't anything they can do to stop it."

"Yeah. Well. I don't buy it." He kissed her forehead and stepped from the bed, finding his jeans. "I'll be ready to leave in five."

"He's going to tell you—"

"Just please get dressed." He snagged his shirt, pulling it over his head. Finding his cell, he pulled up the doctor's phone number, realizing it was after hours. He'd just have to leave a message telling the on-call doctor he was on his way.

And then he'd have to text his family what was going on.

Knowing them, they'd all be five minutes behind for moral support.

And he could certainly use them.

Lorelei climbed up on the hospital gurney, holding Irish's hand as tight as she could.

"It's going to be okay." Irish patted her thigh with his free hand.

She wished she could believe him. Both other times it started with slight spotting and then slowly grew to a steady flow until she became crampy.

And then the bad news came that the fetus was no longer viable.

"Blood pressure is a little high," the nurse said. "But that's common when someone is nervous or in situations such as this."

Lorelei glared at the nurse as if she all but said Lorelei was having a miscarriage, though she knew that was the truth. It didn't matter that both times she'd gone to the bathroom, little to no blood had materialized, nor was she experiencing any cramps; those were just moments away.

"No temperature," the nurse commented. "Oxygen and pulse are good."

"Not to be rude, but unless there is something that is wrong, we don't need the blow-by-blow," Irish said with a harsh tone.

It wasn't deserving, but Lorelei appreciated the sentiment considering her nerves were fried.

She blew in a deep breath and let it out slowly.

"We've got a room for you," the nurse said as she rolled a wheelchair over to Lorelei. "It will be a few minutes before the doctor can get to you."

Irish didn't let go of her hand the entire stroll down the long corridor and around the corner to a private room in the high-risk maternity ward.

"Just climb up on the bed and make yourself comfortable." The nurse handed them a remote. "She can't have anything other than ice chips for now. Can I bring you some?"

"That would be nice." Lorelei took Irish's help as she tried to make herself comfortable, only she couldn't. It wasn't that the bed was all that horrible; it was just that her focus was somewhere else. She shifted from one hip, to the other, only to move again.

"I know this is going to fall on deaf ears, but try to relax."

"Easy for you to say."

"No, it's not." Irish sat on the corner of the bed. He rested his hand on her leg and squeezed gently. "I know you're scared."

"I'm past scared. I'm angry." For ten years, all she wanted was to be a mother and now that hope was once again going to be stolen from her and this time for good. "I can't go through this again."

"We don't know that you are."

She tilted her head. "I know my body, so I know what's happening." She put up her hand. "It always starts slow and in about five hours, things will be very different."

"Lorelei. I think we need to be positive."

She wiped the tears that rolled down her cheeks. "You can be all the positive you want. I prefer to be realistic."

Just then the doctor pulled back the curtain and entered the room. "So, tell me exactly what's going on."

"I'm having a miscarriage," Lorelei said, folding her arms over her chest.

"We don't know that for sure." Irish just had to interject his ridiculous opinion.

"I've been down this road before," she said under her breath.

"You have, but that doesn't mean that's what is happening this time." The doctor lifted her shirt and pressed on her belly. "How much blood was there and are you still bleeding?"

"There was some on the sheets this morning," she said. "But it appears to have stopped."

"That's good," the doctor said. "To be honest, a little spotting is normal during the first trimester."

"Maybe for most woman, but not for me." Lorelei bit back the tears. She knew she shouldn't have allowed herself to feel as though she'd been past the point of no return just because she'd carried longer than the last time. This had been her chance for a child and now it was gone.

And so was her relationship with Irish.

Why would he want to be with her now?

"I can certainly understand why you'd feel that way, but let's start with an ultrasound and we can go from there," the doctor said. "Let me step out for a moment and get the machine. I'll be back in shortly."

"You don't have to sit with me." Lorelei turned away from Irish's kind gaze. She just couldn't deal with him or his feelings. Whatever they might be. Hell, she could barely deal with the up and down of her own. She waffled between rage and utter sadness.

"Don't you dare try to push me away." Irish stood and paced at the foot of the bed. "Ever since we left the house, you've been trying to cut me off at the pass. Well, I won't have it."

She opened her mouth, but snapped it shut right quick when she stared into his dark orbs. "It's not that I'm pushing you away, but you're expecting me to anticipate some miracle or—"

He held up his hand. "Save it." He turned his back and made his way toward the small window and folded his arms. "I don't like it when you get like this."

"Like what? Realistic." She swallowed the thick emotion that had bubbled into her throat. Tears flowed freely down her cheeks. She hated that she was once again reduced to a pathetic woman who couldn't see past her own pain. "Because I refuse to hold on to any kind of a false sense of hope. That's just cruel."

"Until we know for sure, I'm holding on to hope." He turned. "I wish you would too. Kitty says it's good for the baby."

"You need to accept the fact there is no—"

A knock on the door cut off her words. If she were being honest with herself, it was best that she was kept from saying exactly what she was thinking because her thoughts were more than negative.

They were filled with a million *why me's*. Mentally, she had herself on a plane back to North

Carolina and moving on with her life. She had to. She had to forget about Irish and their child that would never be born.

"Let's take a look at what's going on." The doctor rolled the ultrasound machine next to the bed.

Lorelei covered her eyes with her forearm. She sucked in a deep breath, hoping to keep from crying, but it was too late.

"Come on, honey." Irish was at her side in a second. He wrapped his arm around her shoulders. He kissed her temple. "We're both scared, but we have to let the doctor do his job."

"I know," she whispered. "But I can't look. I don't want to see an empty screen with no heartbeat." She shook her head. "I just can't."

"Shhhhh. It's okay. You don't have to look. I will." Irish sat on the edge of the bed and held her free hand, bringing it to his lips.

"Okay, Lorelei. You know the drill. The gel is going to be a little cold." The doctor lifted her shirt while she unhooked her slacks, rolling them down over her hips, keeping her eyes tightly closed.

"Look at me." Irish kissed her temple. "Keep your eyes focused on mine."

"No." She shook her head. "Can we just get this over with, please?"

"We can get started," the doctor said. "Irish, why

don't you focus your attention on the screen."

Lorelei didn't want to see or hear anything. She did her best to tune out her surroundings, ignoring the beeps coming from the machine. "Just tell me when it's over."

Irish could understand Lorelei's concern and he couldn't condemn her behavior. Hell, he wasn't sure if he really wanted to look either, but for different reasons.

He had no idea what he was supposed to be looking for and based on what he could see so far, he had no idea if there was a baby there or not.

And there was no sound.

His heart dropped to his gut.

His first thought was they could try again, but based on Lorelei's anguish, there was no way he could put her through that again.

"Hey, Doc? Can you give us a minute before we finish this exam?"

"Excuse me?" The doctor stopped moving the device over Lorelei's belly and stared at Irish as if he had two heads. "I was just about to show you—"

"It can wait a few minutes."

"I'll be waiting in the hallway. Just let me know

when I can come back in." The doctor wiped off the ultrasound machine and stepped out of the room.

"What's going on?" Lorelei adjusted herself in the bed. "Did you see something? Is the baby gone?"

"I honestly don't know," Irish admitted. "But I have some things I want to say to you before we find out."

She blinked. "Why can't it wait?"

He pushed the portable ultrasound station to the side, making sure she couldn't see the screen, considering she would probably know exactly what she was looking at and he didn't want her to know. Not yet. "Because you need to know that what I'm about to say has nothing to do with the outcome of this ultrasound."

"You're kind of wigging me out here."

He inched up on the bed and took her hands in his. He'd never said this to a woman.

Ever.

Not even Jillian and he did care about her more than he'd ever cared for another girl.

But he hadn't loved her.

Lorelei was a different story.

"No matter what happens with this pregnancy, you need to know how I feel."

"About what?" she asked.

"You." He kissed the back of her hand. "I love you,

Lorelei. I don't know how or when it happened, but I want to make a relationship with you work regardless of what happens."

She clutched her chest. Her jaw slacked open. "But—"

He hushed her by brushing his lips over her mouth. "Either you love me or you don't."

"What about the baby?"

He sucked in a deep breath and let it out slowly. "I want the baby. With everything that I am. But I also want a life with you. I don't know what this ultrasound is going to show. I hope it's positive. But if it's not, that doesn't change how I feel. Now, maybe it's too soon to be talking about trying again, or adopting, because we haven't even discussed getting married or anything like that."

"Are you serious?" She sat up, cupping his cheeks.

"I've never been more serious in my life," he said. "Now, do you love me or not?"

"I love you very much, Irish Whiskey."

He smiled. "You just made me the happiest man in the world."

She wrapped her arms around his body, resting her head on his shoulders. "I think we need to bring the doctor back in and find out what's going on."

"I agree." Irish hopped off the bed and opened the door. "We're ready, Doc."

"Good." The doctor resumed his place on the side of the bed and restarted the ultrasound. "Lorelei, I think you're going to want to open your eyes for this."

"Why?" she asked.

The doctor turned a knob and the sound of a heartbeat and an echo filled the room.

Irish smiled. "Is that the baby's heartbeat?"

The doctor moved the monitor. "It is, but you should know—"

"Is there a problem?" Irish asked.

"Oh, my God." Lorelei bolted to a sitting position.

"What is it? What's wrong?" Irish's heart slammed into the back of his throat. "Lorelei? Are you okay?"

"Is that what I think it is?" She pointed to the screen and glanced between it and the doctor, who nodded.

"Someone want to tell me what the hell is going on?" Irish couldn't stand being the only one in the room who didn't know what the hell was going on.

Lorelei smiled. Tears rolled down her cheeks. "You might need to sit down for this, Daddy."

"So, I'm still going to be a father."

She nodded holding up two fingers. "Times two."

"What does that mean?" he asked.

"Twins. We're having twins."

*I*rish set his son in his crib and lifted his daughter into his arms, kissing the top of her head. He'd never thought he'd find being a parent so rewarding, even though he hadn't slept since they'd brought the twins home two weeks ago.

"Let's go see Mama," he whispered as he handed Elizabeth to Lorelei.

"Do you think these four in the morning feedings will ever end?" Lorelei asked.

He bent over and patted Josh's back as he fussed in his crib. "God, I hope so, but then before we know it, they will be dating and asking for our car keys."

"Bite your tongue." Lorelei shifted in the bed as she breastfed their little girl.

Irish had been looking for the right time to ask

this question, but something always got in the way and if he didn't do it now, then next thing he knew, either one of the twins would need a diaper change, or he'd need a nap.

Or both.

He pulled open his nightstand drawer and snagged the pouch he'd had hidden for weeks. He climbed back into bed, fluffing his pillow, then leaned back. "You know I love you, right?"

"You better." She elbowed him in the side.

He groaned.

"Oh, stop. That didn't hurt."

He chuckled. "No. It didn't but if you say no to this, it will bruise my ego." He held out a diamond ring. "I love you and I want us to be married. What do you say? Make an honest man out of me?"

"You seriously asked me that when I got one of our kids attached to my boob like an appendage?"

He chuckled. "It was now or in the middle of diaper changing or wait until morning and hope we actually had a few moments before I had to leave for work."

"Good point, but you've made it impossible for me to wrap my arms around you and give you a proper yes."

He leaned in and kissed her sweet lips. "Any yes is good enough for me."

"Then, yes. I love you, Irish Whiskey, and I want to spend the rest of my life loving you."

"Deadly Secrets is the best of romance and suspense in one hot read!" *NYT Bestselling Author Jennifer Probst*

"A charming setting and a steamy couple heat up the pages in a suspenseful story I couldn't put down!" *NY Times and USA today Bestselling Author Donna Grant*

"Jen Talty's books will grab your attention and pull you into a world of relatable characters, strong personalities, humor, and believable storylines. You'll laugh, you'll cry, and you'll rush to get the next book she releases!" Natalie Ann USA Today Bestselling Author

"I positively loved *In Two Weeks*, and highly recommend it. The writing is wonderful, the story is fantastic, and the characters will keep you coming back for more. I can't wait to get my hands on future installments of the NYS Troopers series." *Long and Short Reviews*

"*In Two Weeks* hooks the reader from page one. This is a fast paced story where the development of the romance grabs you emotionally and the suspense keeps you sitting on the edge of your chair. Great characters, great writing, and a believable plot that can be a warning to all of us." *Desiree Holt, USA Today Bestseller*

"*Dark Water* delivers an engaging portrait of wounded hearts as the memorable characters take you on a healing journey of love. A mysterious death brings danger and intrigue into the drama, while sultry passions brew into a believable plot that melts the reader's heart. Jen Talty pens an entertaining romance that grips the heart as the colorful and dangerous story unfolds into a chilling ending." *Night Owl Reviews*

"This is not the typical love story, nor is it the typical mystery. The characters are well rounded and interesting." *You Gotta Read Reviews*

"*Murder in Paradise Bay* is a fast-paced romantic thriller with plenty of twists and turns to keep you guessing until the end. You won't want to miss this one..." *USA Today bestselling author Janice Maynard*

ABOUT THE AUTHOR

Jen Talty is the *USA Today* Bestselling Author of Contemporary Romance, Romantic Suspense, and Paranormal Romance. In the fall of 2020, her short story was selected and featured in a 1001 Dark Nights Anthology. She is currently contracted to write in the *With Me in Seattle* series by Kristen Proby with Lady Boss Press, as well as Susan Stoker's *Special Forces: Operation Alpha* and Elle James's *Brotherhood Protectors.*

Regardless of the genre, her goal is to take you on a ride that will leave you floating under the sun with warmth in your heart. She writes stories about broken heroes and heroines who aren't necessarily looking for romance, but in the end, they find the kind of love books are written about :).

She first started writing while carting her kids to one hockey rink after the other, averaging 170 games per year between 3 kids in 2 countries and 5 states. Her first book, IN TWO WEEKS was originally published in 2007. In 2010 she helped form a publishing company (Cool Gus Publishing) with *NY Times* Bestselling Author Bob Mayer where she ran the technical side of the business through 2016.

Jen is currently enjoying the next phase of her life… the empty nester! She and her husband reside in Jupiter, Florida.

Grab a glass of vino, kick back, relax, and let the romance roll in…

Sign up for my Newsletter (https://dl.bookfunnel. com/82gm8b9k4y) where I often give away free books before publication.

Join my private Facebook group (https://www.facebook. com/groups/191706547909047/) where I post exclusive excerpts and discuss all things murder and love!

Never miss a new release. Follow me on Amazon:amazon.com/author/jentalty

And on Bookbub: bookbub.com/authors/jen-talty

ALSO BY JEN TALTY

Club Temptation

SWEET TEMPTATION

Legacy Series

DARK LEGACY

With Me In Seattle

INVESTIGATE WITH ME

SAIL WITH ME

The Monroes

COLOR ME YOURS

COLOR ME SMART

COLOR ME FREE

COLOR ME LUCKY

COLOR ME ICE

It's all in the Whiskey

JOHNNIE WALKER

GEORGIA MOON

JACK DANIELS

THE LOST SISTER

THE LOST SOLDIER

THE LOST SOUL

THE LOST CONNECTION

A Spin-Off Series: Witches Academy Series

THE NEW ORDER

Special Forces Operation Alpha

BURNING DESIRE

BURNING KISS

BURNING SKIES

BURNING LIES

BURNING HEART

BURNING BED

REMEMBER ME ALWAYS

The Brotherhood Protectors

Out of the Wild

ROUGH JUSTICE

ROUGH AROUND THE EDGES

ROUGH RIDE

ROUGH EDGE

ROUGH BEAUTY

SPRING FLING

SUMMER'S GONE

WINTER WEDDING

Witches and Werewolves

LADY SASS

ALL THAT SASS

Coming soon! NEON SASS

Coming soon! PAINTING SASS